"Well, this meteor-"

"*Comet.*"

"-*Comet* better be worth it."

Half of their quaint town has gathered to witness the comet passing by. With such a clear night, they're bound to get a good view. Some have started a bonfire to keep people warm and set up stalls. Most are from nearby shops selling jewellery and books, but some are food. Her mouth waters at the smell of homemade burgers and chips drifting from the nearest one. Courtney wants to see the comet first, then worry about eating later.

"Why did we have to sit so far from the fire?" Jason continues to grumble. "It's cold up here."

Courtney rolls her eyes. "I told you, it's packed down there."

"And?"

"The view will be better from up here."

They're sat on a damp blanket a little way up the hill. Everyone else is crowded at the bottom, happily chatting away and eating while waiting for the comet.

Tori's stomach growls again. "I hope they have enough burgers left."

Courtney flashes her a smile that makes her heart thump. "There will be plenty. Have you seen the amount of people visiting from out of town? They'll be well stocked."

"Yeah, you're right."

Courtney smiles through her veil of black hair, making her blush. She could stand a few minutes longer up here if it meant hanging out with her a while longer.

"How big is this comet?"

And hanging out with *him*.

Jason, Courtney's stepbrother, is a thorn in her side. He goes wherever they go, no matter how much she protests. It gets grating to have to deal with him all the time. Especially as he's a year older than them.

Courtney resists another eye roll. "*Big.* We should be able to see the trail it leaves."

Jason nods slowly and then looks down at the bonfire. He instantly recoils and pulls his hood over his face. "Shit."

"What's up?" Tori asks.

"Guys from my school."

"The bullies?"

He nods slowly. "Ugh. Of course, they would be here."

As annoying as she finds him, she doesn't like to see him get picked on. "Do you want to go?"

He peeks out of the hole in his hood. "Can we?"

"We haven't seen the comet yet!" Courtney groans.

"I don't want to get picked on, Court."

NEPHILIM

compiled by

STACEY JAINE MCINTOSH

IRON FAERIE
PUBLISHING

Cover designed by
Lafae Cover Designs
www.facebook.com/lafaecoverdesigns

Iron Faerie Publishing
www.ironfaeriepublishing.com

ISBN: 9798876208972

Printed in the United States of America

First Printing September 2023

CONTENTS

FALSE COMET

JESSICA TURNBULL

Tori brings her legs closer to her chest, wishing she was nearer the fire. Her thin denim jacket is doing little to keep out the night chill. Her eyes dart up to the sky, which is an inky black smeared with purple and blue hues. There are hardly any clouds in the sky, their small wisps drift across the moon, barely shielding the stars.

"How much longer?" The boy next to them grunts, drawing his coat zipper even higher up his neck.

The girl beside Tori sighs. "I don't know. It's a natural event, they tend to run whenever they want."

"You knew they'd be here, it's not a surprise."

Before Tori can wade into their argument, people starting shouting and pointing upwards. Several bright lights are streaking across the sky. They shoot over their heads in quick succession, darting across the sky like bullets. Whites and pale oranges fill the blackness as more and more flash by.

"I thought the comet was supposed to be huge?" Jason grumbles.

Courtney gapes as she stares upwards. "It is. This is a meteor shower."

Tori shrugs. "It's still pretty."

"Woah, look at that one!" Jason points at the sky, pulling his hood down completely.

A light brighter than the rest streaks over the moon. It leaves a fiery orange trail behind it. Unlike the others, this one is angled downwards. The three of them can only watch as it gets bigger and bigger as it hurtles towards them. It crashes into the forest not far from them, barely letting off a small boom as it does so. She would have thought that it would have made a louder noise, or a bigger impact.

"That one crashed!" Tori breathes, accidentally grabbing Courtney's hand.

The other girl doesn't seem to notice. "No way! A comet

4

wouldn't just *crash*."

"You said it was a meteor a minute ago!" Jason argues. "A shooting star that fell out of the sky, how cool is that?"

Below them, the other town residents are whispering to themselves and pointing in the direction it crashed. Tori feels her heart swell with excitement. Nothing happens around here, and now a shooting star falls near them?

"It's *not* a shooting star!" Courtney growls. "Stars don't fall out of the sky."

"Whatever it is, we should go after it."

Tori, unable to stop herself, speaks before looking at Courtney. "Yes! We need to check it out!"

"What?" Courtney shakes her head and Tori goes red. "No way, too dangerous."

"It's just a meteor," Jason grunts. "How bad could it be?"

"It's obviously going to be boiling hot and full of radiation, it's a no."

Already people are starting to leave, following the general direction the meteor landed. As much as Tori wants to agree with Courtney, her heart is pulling her towards an adventure. She doesn't want everyone to see the meteor and talk about it for weeks while she hung back. There's no fun in that.

She starts jogging down the hill. "Come on, let's go!"

Jason excitedly bounces after her while Courtney trails

behind them, her lips drawn into a thin line.

This will be worth it, I promise.

What Tori hadn't expected to do tonight was trek through a forest. Her clothes are more for comfort than stomping around in mud and getting twigs in her hair. With her naturally tight brunette curls, she's worried that she will get snagged by a low branch. Just ahead of them is another group, all significantly older than them. It's not just teenagers who want to see the meteor.

"This is great! You were right, Court, this is really fun!" Jason beams as he jumps on exposed tree roots.

"This isn't what I meant by fun," Courtney grunts as one of her stilettos gets stuck in the mud. "I meant watching the comet and then having a burger by the fire. Not traipsing through the woods at eleven o'clock at night."

Tori drops back to help her out of the mud. "I know this isn't what you had planned, but it's still cool, right? I mean, there's a meteor out there."

Courtney shrugs her shoulders. "I guess."

"When are we ever going to get an opportunity like this again? Even if it is some kind of space debris, that's still cool, right?"

The girl smiles slightly at this. "Yeah. I guess you're right."

There are shouts from up ahead, but they sound disappointed. Jason rushes ahead, not bothering to wait for the girls. They arrive seconds after him to the crowd dispersing.

"Aww..." Jason moans. "I thought there would be something cool."

There's a small crater in front of them, the edges still sizzling. The soggy ground around it has almost completely dried up, and several trees have split around it from the impact. This also seems strange, as it barely made a sound when it landed.

Tori feels stupid for convincing Courtney to come out now. "Maybe it burned up in the atmosphere."

"No way," Courtney grunts. "If it had, there wouldn't be an impact site. Something landed here."

More spectators come up behind them, though leave shortly after. Soon, the three of them are the only ones out there. Jason wanders around the crater, careful not to get too close. There's still quite a bit of heat coming from it, and none of them want to go home and explain to their parents how they got burned.

Jason suddenly stops and wanders back into the forest a bit. "Hey, I think I've found something!"

Courtney rolls her eyes. "How about the path home?"

The two of them follow him back into the trees. The ground underneath them is dry as a bone, and the leaves on the trees have been singed. There are marks on the floor that are too big for a small animal, more like something large dragged itself.

"I don't like this," Tori shivers. "I think we should go back."

"Hold on," Jason calls from ahead. "I think I see something."

Even Courtney seems curious now, no longer complaining each time her heels sink into the mud. "Maybe an animal dragged it away."

"If we find it, we'll be the talk of the town." Jason turns around momentarily to grin.

The silence in the forest is starting to make Tori paranoid. Why aren't the owls out? Why does it feel like there could be something hiding in the trees?

Jason suddenly drops to his knees as a low growl echoes through the trees. Tori feels her blood turn to ice as the sound continues for a few seconds. Whatever animal is in the forest, its big, and it doesn't want to be disturbed.

"We should go." She hisses under her breath.

Jason is already crawling forward. The tree in the front of them shakes and she stifles a gasp. A large shape moves past it, and the sound of crunching can be heard.

"It's just eating something, let's go."

Courtney, braver than both of them, touches the tree and peers around it. An orange light blinds them momentarily, making Tori stumble backwards.

"Come see." She breathes.

As much as every instinct in her body tells her to run, the soothing voice of the girl makes her press forward. Jason is standing up again now, peering around the other side of the trunk. Courtney moves aside so Tori can see. When her fingers brush against the bark, there's another burst of orange light, but this one barely lasts a second.

When the light dies down, she has to cover her mouth with her hand to prevent herself from crying out. There's a body on the floor, but it isn't human. Six white feathery wings sprout from its back, dirtied by the mud. Its face is just a white glow, so bright that the features underneath can't be seen. But the light isn't uncomfortable; it's almost as if it tells her eyes not to focus on the face. Its torso has been ripped open, and a golden liquid oozes from its wounds. It must be at least ten feet tall, though its legs are bent and broken.

And then there's the creature that caught it.

It's about eight feet tall and has six wings sprouting from its back, but they don't look right. The feathers look so dry

9

and dull that they could crumble under just a touch. The wings themselves are drooped, and don't look healthy enough to carry it off the ground. Its skin is a sickly grey, covered in black splotches that look like bruises. There's a small rag around its waist to cover its dignity. It looks like a cross between the corpse beside it and a human.

The creature kneels over the dead one and digs around in its torso. Its grey hand pulls out a handful of the golden ooze, which emits a bright orange glow that forces her to close her eyes. It then shoves its entire fist in its mouth, its swollen dark tongue lapping at its thin fingers.

"What is that?" Jason croaks, backing away.

"It looks like an angel." Courtney whispers.

"That is one *fucked* up angel."

"The dead one. The alive one kind of looks like an angel," She crinkles her nose. "I don't really know what it is."

"And how would you know what an angel looks like?"

"Humans don't fall out of the sky. Angels can, the Bible said so."

Tori pulls away quickly, not wanting to watch the hideous scene anymore. There are more orange glows behind them that increase in ferocity. Eventually, the three of them back off a few feet from the tree.

She grabs Courtney's arm. "Let's go, please."

Courtney yanks her arm away. "No, I want to watch."

"Watch what? It's eating something."

"An angel. It must have been the thing that fell."

"And the other one? Did that fall too?"

Courtney goes quiet. "I think that one was already here."

Tori's stomach lurches. The thought of that thing already being here makes her head hurt. Why is it here? Why is it eating that angel-thing? Why did that angel-thing fall out of the sky?

Jason approaches the tree once more, and she desperately wants to call him back. He peers around once the light has died down and falls back with a squeak. The tree shakes and then snaps as weight is put on it from one side. Splinters go flying in all directions, and there's a loud crack as the bark finally buckles. The grey creature steps over it, its mouth covered in the golden ooze. The gold colour starts to die out until it's a clear liquid. Its brown eyes focus on each of them, and the corners of its lips turn upwards in a snarl.

"What is this thing?" Jason screams, tripping over his own feet as he tries to get away.

Now that it's facing them, its features are surprisingly human. Its chest is covered in a thick mat of dark hair, as well as its head and neck. If it weren't for the sheer size of it and the wings, it could easily pass as a human.

11

Courtney falls backwards, creating a loud squelch as she slaps into the mud. The creature is drawn by the two of them moving, but Tori is frozen to the spot.

Jason clutches the nearest tree, shooting the girls a panicked glance. "I'm out of here!"

Before he can even move, the creature swats at him with a long arm. He can barely scream before the wind is knocked out of his body. The creature then closes the gap between them in two steps. Jason opens his mouth, but nothing comes out. A clammy hand grabs Tori's arm and she yelps without meaning to.

"Help me!" Jason tries to scramble away from the monster, but it places a foot over his chest to prevent him from escaping.

"We need to leave." Courtney hisses in her ear.

Tori's eyes bulge. "What? We can't!"

"That thing already has him. We can get away."

Courtney's brown eyes are filled with fear. It's clear that self-preservation has all but kicked in at this point. Tori can't deny that she also feels the same pull to run.

"Court! Tori-"

Jason is cut off when the creature lifts its foot and then slams it down. A hiss of air escapes his mouth as the foot goes through his ribcage. Blood spurts everywhere and Tori can't hold back her scream. The creature spins to glare at her, its nostrils flaring.

"Tori!"

Courtney is already running, having dropped her arm. Tori glances once more at Jason's body before scrambling after her. Loud stomps behind them signify that the creature is following. With its long legs it doesn't need to run, it can keep a good distance between them. The sound of rushing water hits her ears, and she watches Courtney dart off to the side.

"Don't leave me!" She screams.

It's no use, Courtney has already disappeared into the darkness. The creature is now completely interested in Tori, who has no choice but to stumble around in the dark. She can no longer hear Courtney's footsteps, drowned out by the sound of water.

The river! Can this thing swim?

There have been harsh rains recently, which have made the river swell beyond its banks. The ground starts to get stickier the closer she gets to the water. Without thinking, she splashes into the river itself. When it's up to her knees she can feel the strong current trying to tug her downstream. She ignores the uncomfortable feeling of water flooding her trainers to look back.

The creature hasn't stopped.

It hesitates for a second before stepping into the water. Its large feet sink into the muddy bank, leaving gaping holes. Tori tries to go out further, but the river tugs at her clothes hungrily. If she goes too far, she'll get caught in the current. Luckily, behind her is a thick tree branch, which has been caught between the rocks. She clings to it as the water rushes past, hoping she doesn't slip.

She waves her arms at the creature. "Go away! The water is too strong!"

If it could understand her, it makes no notion of it. Instead, it continues moving forward, its feet sloshing in the mud and silt. She can see the force of the river is even forcing its body along with the water. It gets closer and closer, and she starts to panic.

I need to get out of here!

There are only two directions she can take, further out into the water or towards the creature. She can either drown or be killed by this thing.

Its large body topples slightly as it wades out above its knees. It's then she notices that despite its enormous size, its legs and arms are thinner than they're supposed to be. They aren't in proportion with the rest of its body. Could they be weaker?

14

With a deep breath, she shimmies around the branch until she's at the far end. She then stretches herself out, as far as she dares. Mouthfuls of dirty water make her want to gag, but she perseveres.

"Come get me then!" She spits when she gets a breath of clean air.

The creature continues to advance, either not noticing or not caring about the current tugging at its thighs. The deeper it gets, the more its body starts to sway. It gets close enough to reach a hand out to her, sacrificing some of its balance. Some of its wings get drenched in the water, and the force of the current yanks them out to full length. They must be two metres long each, and the river forces the wings to stretch further and further out. The creature tries to regain itself, but the heavy wings are now completely dragged under and getting pulled along with the current. It tries to retreat, but the waterlogged wings are too heavy.

Tori coils herself around the tree branch as it topples over momentarily. Behind it, she can see some sort of debris slam into its back, knocking it over. That's enough time for the current to suck it under completely. There's a roar before its face disappears under the murky blackness. Tori shivers and squints, trying to see if it will pop back up and get her, anyway. Further downstream she hears another roar and lets out a sigh of relief.

The current is still tugging at her body, and she can feel herself getting tired. With the last of her strength, she moves along the branch until she's back on the bloated riverbank. Only when she's safely back on her feet does she look up.

There are more stars shooting across the sky, though none of them touch the Earth.

THE WINDS OF CHANGE

EMILY SHARP

Long ago, in a time when the prairies and mountains stood bare; alone and vast, in a time when the forests stood tall and rich, and the animals ruled the earth with Man that walked alongside them, there was a noble and respectful tribe who gave back to the Earth what they took from it.

This tribe had all that they needed and lived in harmony and without fear or want. They abided by the laws of nature and respected the earth and its creatures. The mighty bison were plentiful, as were the fish and the deer. The plants healed them, dyed their   clothes, and provided food. The people of the tribe worshipped the Spirits of the Earth and worshipped their ways. They were in rhythm with the earth and all she had to offer.

There was in this tribe a powerful and knowledgeable medicine man. His knowledge had been passed down from his father and his father before him, all the way from when the Great Spirits had shown their people the ways. The Medicine Man blessed and healed the tribe and its people, led the dances, and taught the children myths and legends of their people around campfires. The stars listened too when he told the tales of his people; twinkling happily, as they remembered such times.

Despite all his power and knowledge, the Medicine Man and his wife could not produce children to carry on his line. Many a babe did not make the journey from the Spirit World to our world, and many a child did not last more than a breath or a moon. As the Medicine Man and his wife grew in age, so did their hopes wane of ever having a child to carry on Medicine Man's proud line of knowledge.

Until one season, the Medicine Man's wife's belly was swollen with yet another babe and the spirits called to the Medicine Man to join them for council. The Medicine Man obediently went, leaving his pregnant wife to rest alone in the safety of their wigwam. The Spirits' council took many hours and, before long, the pregnant wife became restless and uncomfortable in her state. She decided to collect some flowers and herbs to offer the spirits in order to ease her pains, the other tribesmen and women greeting her as she headed into the forest.

Before long, the Medicine Man arrived home with a heavy conscience. The Spirits had foretold that his wife would indeed bear another babe and that they would be blessed with a child to carry on the legacy. But, for such a substantial gift from the Spirit World, something of equal worth had to be given in return and the life essence had to be refilled and balanced accordingly.

The Medicine Man came back to find the wigwam he shared with his beloved wife empty. As he searched the village, the tribes people told of seeing his wife head alone to the forest to collect herbs. Suddenly a child's wail sounded clearly and piercingly through the night, coming from the forest. The tribe immediately sped towards the noise as one; the Medicine Man on swift feet leading his people. They followed the wail to find a newly born babe alone in the clearing. One look told the Medicine Man what the Spirits had meant , and he fell to his knees. There was a still bitter moments of silence before he began crying out for his cherished wife's spirit to come back to him. The village people let him be one with his grief and pain unabated until one of the wiser hunters finally placed the babe in his arms.

Even though their payment had been high, the Spirits had finally given the medicine man his heir.

***

The young girl grew up strong, quick, and clever. Much loved by her father and her tribe, she was aptly named Tehya, meaning "Precious One". She followed her father everywhere and, much to his delight, picked up his knowledge and skills quicker than anyone could anticipate. Before long, she was joining him in leading ceremonies and healing. She spread great pride and joy throughout the tribe and made her father feel love again in the absence of his soul mate, Tehya's mother. Many nights she would hear her father talking to her mother's spirit, telling her of all that Tehya had achieved and would achieve, and her amazing grasp and appetite for his wisdom and craft. Tehya would listen and long to speak to her mother too, but she had not yet been gifted with the ability to commune with the Spirits, the only aspect of her father's craft she had not yet mastered.

Soon, the season came when Tehya was of age and it was agreed by the village elders, that in order to follow her path and honour her father's line, she would undertake a Vision Quest. Some of the males of the tribe were seen to disagree, but they did not   voice their opinions against the elders. With permission and encouragement from her father, she agreed. Tehya would be the first female of the tribe to undergo a Vision Quest, and the first female in her family line to follow the role of her fathers and forefathers. In hushed corners whilst preparing food, skins, and the like, many a woman of the tribe buzzed excitedly, wondering what that could possibly mean for the future for their daughters, and prayed to the Spirits for Tehya to have the strength to complete her quest.

The night came, and a hush fell over the tribe as they gathered to watch Tehya prepare and begin her quest. Dressed in her ceremonial robes, her father performing the necessary rites leading her from childhood to adulthood, she looked every ounce as noble and deserving as any young male. It was decreed that where she was found as a babe – in the clearing of the woods – would be the place of her quest.

The tribe followed at a distance, the women chanting and singing prayers of safety, speed, and clarity as Tehya strode confidently after her father. As they approached the clearing, all fell silent. Those who were there that night swept silent tears of remembrance, including her father. He performed the final chant and handed Tehya her skin pouch of spirit tea. Their eyes met, for the final time as child to father, before she became a woman and the tribe left her alone to begin her quest.

Tehya

I sit alone.

The forest's music surrounds me, swimming. It buzzes with life and sweet promises. I am elated and ready. I have been waiting for this moment my whole life. It is time to follow in my father's footsteps and live out my life's path.

The breeze caresses me softly; encouraging my spirit to be free of its earthly bonds. The moon and stars twinkle in excitement, watching, waiting. The evening star, bold and bright, asserts dominance over his domain, blessing me with his presence and approval. The earth is tingling with anticipation, as am I. I know deep in my soul that it is time.

My spirit tea is bitter, strong. Not any taste I have ever had before. My father brewed it in   secret, as is tradition. It was the first time I had not been a company to him preparing something for ceremony or otherwise. As encouraged, I had fasted before the ceremony and the tea slid to my belly like a snake and waited, coiled, to begin its magic.

I am not scared. Fear is not something we know in my tribe. We respect the bear and the wolf, and acknowledge

22

their power and strength, but do not fear them, as we understand them. As a child, I had heard stories of Wendigoes and water spirits that were worth our fear, as they were evil and unpredictable, but we had never known those spirits to come to our tribe or even near it.

I looked around at the clearing I had been found in, and for countless times, recollected the story of my birth and wondered what happened to my mother. My father had explained the will of the Spirits when I was very young, and I had accepted it, as he had, but I did not carry the same sadness as he did. I had never known my mother, so I could not mourn her. All the mothers in the tribe were my mother. My lost brothers were made up for by the tribe's sons and daughters and my father was both parents in one. I cannot carry sadness for that which I did not know or experience when I have been blessed with so much. Though, something in me did yearn to know my mother and my siblings.

I drank the rest of my tea and wondered whether I would be blessed with the ability to commune with the Spirit World. The mixture suddenly gripped and clenched my stomach in a pain like my woman's pain, causing me to bend over, clutching at my belly. The spasm ran through me again, and as I tried to sit up straight against it, my head swam. Beads of sweat formed on my brow and hairline, and saliva pooled in my mouth. The clearing ahead of me began to spin ever so slowly that I almost did not notice it. I tried to focus my eyes as a birch tree's black markings began to drip and bleed into one another. I closed my eyes, remembering my father's warnings that the Spirits would play trickster games with my vision and the earth around me before they made their appearance. I smiled against the pain and my head that felt like swirling liquid in a drinking skin.

I opened my eyes. The colours of the forest chattered excitedly, all contesting for my attention at once. The ground rippled as water. The leaves of the forest floor crawled and chewed each other. The trees waved and danced, laughing playfully, as they dipped and swayed in my vision. I laughed with them and heard the stars echo me. I looked above, losing myself in the beauty of it all. The night sky expanded, enveloped me; speckling the blackness was a seething mass of stars, welcoming me, chasing me, and running from me, leading and following. As I played with them gleefully, one fell from the sky and towards earth with a tail of fire. I ran after it, laughing joyfully as I sped through the trees to keep up; almost flying as my feet barely touched the earth.

The star landed just ahead of me, its fire going out as it hit the earth. I pushed aside the branches between me and the star, and in front of me, lay not a fallen star but a large male

24

hunter. He lay where he had hit the ground, unconscious. He was dressed in the most vibrant coloured feathers and skins I had ever seen and wore beads and shells that I could not recognise; I ran to him and kneeling next to him, looked into his face. The Spirits were still playing with my vision and warped his features slightly. I could see that he was of very noble and handsome birth, and he was of a much grander stature than I had seen of any man before. His breathing was slow and shallow, so I lay a hand on his brow and I knew immediately that he was afflicted with an illness. Upon my touch, he opened his eyes and looked up at me. He had kept the stars in his eyes; they sparkled at me with love and wisdom.

"I am of a sickness, not of our people, medicine woman."

His voice was all around us, yet in my head. It was soft and kind. I knew he was not speaking the language of my people, yet I understood.

"Only you can heal me. But you must travel to the Spirit World and ask my spirit for the remedy, as in this form on this plane I do not know the sickness yet, and neither do your people."

I could see in his eyes that his life essence was fading and being eaten by this sickness.

"My father knows all sicknesses and all remedies…"

25

"Not this one. This is not of your people. This is something that will be brought on swift wings upon the wind, attacking and devouring your people. You must go. You alone, precious one, will heal me. It is your path."

With that, he lifted a feeble, strained arm and pointed just beyond us. As he did so, a cavern opened up in the earth where he was pointing. I looked back at him, but he had succumbed to unconsciousness again.

I stood carefully, my spirits still enjoying their games with my vision and rattling my head. I walked into the cavern, which swallowed me easily. It was the perfect height for me to walk down, neither steep nor flat, yet graduated down at a tilt that was easy and comfortable. As I walked, I went further and further into the earth; deeper and deeper. My feet were not sore nor were my legs tired, no matter how far I walked. Yet, it felt like many moons, but no more than a few breaths as I came to the end of the tunnel.

In front of me was a great cavern of indescribable beauty and light. And in it, the most amazingly perfect village, yet bigger than I had ever seen, spread across the cavern's landscape. There were crops growing in abundance, trees with fruit, more bountiful and larger in size than I had seen before. Everything and everyone shone with a brilliant light and colour as the sun touches a rippling body of water, yet had a smoke-like haze.

Suddenly, a small toddler waddled in front of me and held its fat arms up. I looked into his face and I knew the babe. As I held him close, he felt familiar, although I had never seen him before. His mother then came towards me laughing and smiling; she glowed and radiated love with every step. A throng of small infants plodded after her and clutched at the bottom of her skirts, and she had another very young one in a pack on her back.

"He's been waiting for his sister. We all have."

I looked into her face and knew instantly, without any doubt… It was my mother.

I put the child down and fell into her embrace. I felt her emotion and soul more than I felt her actual form, but it felt complete all the same. I wept, the tears on her shoulder dripped through her ethereal form. She allowed me to feel what I needed to and then stood back.

"What you seek is new to your world."

I nodded, understanding her repeated words from the fallen hunter.

"From the North East, the winds of change will come on pale wings and with it new disease: fear and greed."

With her words, I felt the new sensation of fear prickle and awaken up my spine. She saw it too. "It will not be in your lifetime my child, but you must carry on the legacy of your father and your father's father. You must bring these remedies to our world for your children and their children to be ready for when it comes."

She stepped away from me, gesturing to a garden next to an elegant and colourful wigwam. I had seen some of the herbs   before, but not all of them. They glowed but lost some of their light as my mother picked them. She bound and wound them tight in a way I had seen my father do. She wrapped them in a neat skin, handing them to me. "When you get to your world, you will have the knowledge of how to use them."

I nodded but thought of the hunter. My mother understood without me having to speak. "Come, you will meet his spirit."

She took me through the dazzling village and into the most elegant wigwam of them all. It was embroidered and patterned with the evening star and its colours. It shone brighter and glittered like the sun on fresh snow. She led me to the doorway and placed a hand on my shoulder. "This is where I leave you, my child. Your path only has room for one set of footsteps: yours."

With that, she turned and disappeared like smoke through sunlight. I longed to stay with her and learn more from her, to be held by her again, but I understood my duty and knew what I had to do.

I entered the wigwam and saw the mighty and handsome hunter sitting on a high seat waiting for me. His spirit was brighter than the others I had seen in the village and had nobleness to it that I had never known in my tribe or any others. His presence humbled me. I imagined even tribal elders would bow at his feet, so I did so.

He smiled and gestured me to rise. "Thank you for following this path, Tehya."

He looked more like a star here than when was disguised as a hunter; even his skin shone, like that of a fish or lizard.

"It is my path to follow."

My father had versed me in speaking with Spirits, as was a tradition before my quest, and now I was thankful for it.

"You have come for the remedy to heal the unknown illness that comes on the winds of the North East."

I nodded.

"But you cannot. The disease that comes cannot be cured by your father's knowledge or the knowledge that came from his father before him because it is not of this land."

He got up and approached me, holding out his arms, radiating brilliance, his eyes noting the skin of herbs my mother had given me.

He smiled. "Yes, they will cure the flesh, but not the mind. Those that come on pale wings are infected with much more than a disease of the body, but of the heart and the soul." He looked off into the distance and was still for a time before carrying   on. "It is time for you to return to your world now. Heal my flesh of that world so I may return to the sky and you and your people will be rewarded." As he came again towards me, the air around us got brighter and brighter until a bright white light was all I could see. I closed my eyes against it and felt everything around me fall away.

When I opened them again, I was standing over the hunter in his human form back in the woods. I looked behind me, the hole had closed up. I knelt beside the hunter again. He was as handsome as he was in the spirit world, but no longer glowed brilliantly or had skin that shone.

I felt the Spirits breathe life into me and take over my body and movements. It was as if I were watching through my own eyes and I could feel what I was doing, but could not control my actions. I was tending to the hunter with knowledge that I did not know I possessed. I used each herb, plant, and flower in the wrap I had been given, naturally knowing the amount and how to squeeze or strip each one of its juice or seed. When I had finished with the mixture, I placed it in the hunter's mouth, and upon swallowing it, he woke.

He looked at me with more gratitude and adoration than anyone had ever given me before. He stood, taking my hands into his own, and raised me with him. He towered above me, and his great dress and feathers shone; emblazoned with vigour once more, he smiled.

"You now have the knowledge and the abilities you seek. Take with you what you have learnt and let it be some remedy against the changing of the times." He looked up at the night sky. "I must go back to where I belong, but know that in return for your kindness, I will always watch over you and your people." With that again, his brightness began to fill everything around us. As the light shone brighter I closed my eyes and no longer felt his presence. When I opened my eyes again, I was standing in the clearing where I started, alone.

I took the knowledge back to my tribe and prepared them with the words of my mother and the great star-hunter. The seeds and roots I had left over took to the earth well and I passed on their uses to my children to pass on to theirs after that. As promised, the evening star shone ever brightly and watched over me and my people.

The winds from the North East would not change us just yet.

EAST OF THE GODS SPINE

BAREND NIEUWSTRATEN III

Something was wrong. Korgorun was alone in the mountains where he and his small clan of loyal orcs had laid to sleep for the night. Though it looked different. Its paths and passes seemed barely traversable, made even more perilous through narrowing, steepness, and detachment. Something had warped the terrain. When he looked up, it seemed neither night nor day, and the sky was purple, filled with black swirling clouds. There was only one moon in the sky, and it was yellow and broken, with pieces of it scattered across the unfamiliar sky.

"Where am I?" the orc demanded, his voice echoing out.

"Where I have summoned you," a voice responded from behind.

Korgorun reached for his axe, ready in his hands as he turned, swinging by the time he was facing them. A hand caught the wooden shaft between his own as he faced a mighty orc before him who smiled and nodded. He was no ordinary orc. Dark skin, under which red veins glowed, eyes of total blackness, a crown of grey metal fixed with ram horns, and red stained dragonbone armour.

"You swing your axe in the middle of an answer you demanded," the stronger orc said, holding him at bay. "Impatient, like your mother."

Korgorun eased his shoulders. The figure before him fit a familiar description. "Father?"

The black-eyed demigod nodded as he twisted the large axe to examine its crude blade. "Stone?" He grunted on the verge of disapproval. "You know the men west of these mountains carry swords and axes of bronze, having eradicated those before them who bore weapons and armour of copper. Then there's the men making purchase on the far coast, to the east, who also come with such arms and armour."

"They still have to get close enough to use them,"

33

Korgorun defiantly answered, before thinking to show reverence. He knelt on one knee, releasing the axe. "My lord, Ochius, son of Grimult." From there he spied upon the demigod's hips the broad knives made of some purple metal. He recalled his mother claiming the material only existed in the void where his father had domain. "Is this your realm?"

"It is the realm of many, but I dwell here, yes," Ochius said, circling his knelt son. "This is Nihrius. The place where those touched by magic go when they sleep. As I have brought you here as you sleep. For my name has been called by the voices of our mortal kin, in places where I and my father are sought. They call for aid, and I am sending you in my stead. For that is why I made you and your kind. Mightier than most because the blood of Grimult has been passed down to you."

"I will do what you command," Korgorun promised, still kneeling. "I ask only that you bestow some blessing upon my axe, in return."

"Stone and wood have served the orc well since before the time of keeping. But a new age is upon us. A second since that of stone. Do as I bid and a weapon befitting a higher mortal as yourself shall grace your hands."

Korgorun nodded. "Command me."

"Go north when you wake. Two days travel through this

very mountain range. The village of Cru-Gol-Yr sits. It is there that their chief has called for my aid. He has heard my voice, and I have named you as their deliverance. Rise and go."

Korgorun made to stand, but instead woke. Surrounded once more by those who followed him under a dark blue sky, moments before the dawn. "Wake," he loudly commanded them. "My father has visited upon me. A quest is upon us."

The orcs who followed Korgorun did so precisely because of whose blood flowed through his veins. Ochius, the demigod offspring of their god, Grimult and a mortal orc warrior who once warred with the men west of the Gods Spine Mountains. The Mud Queen, she was known in legend. In turn, Ochius had laid with several mortals to make protectors who would lead no tribe and wear no crowns. Sworn only to command a trusted few to aid those who called upon their godly forebears. It was the first time Korgorun had been called upon. Still young, he had only ever patrolled the mountains for humans who made to sneak through them.

To hear word of one of their two gods, the orcs who followed him were enamoured. They asked many questions on their journey north, varying little from the theme of how he looked and sounded. Korgorun could not begrudge them, as tiresome as it grew. For he too felt greatly honoured by the visitation. His first command issued by the one who made him. The first time he faced him, while old enough to remember.

When they came upon the village, Korgorun expected to see a place besieged by humans, but instead found a peaceful encampment well protected by the surrounding rock with homes made of rock, bone, and hide. Orc children played, goats and boars wandered about crude enclosures, and older orcs trained the youthful in the use of wooden cudgels, and stone axes. As Korgorun approached with his six loyal followers, those guarding the village called attention to the approaching visitors.

"Is this Cru-Gol-Yr?" Korgorun asked, when close enough.

Widening their elbows, to ready themselves for a fight, the guards gave a single nod.

"I must speak with your chief," Korgorun instructed. "Fetch him or lead me to him. He is waiting for me."

"What is your name?" a voice called from far behind the guards protecting the entrance. An older orc emerged from one of the hide tents wearing goat horns upon his shoulders and a headband of woven hide strips.

"I am Korgorun. You called upon my father, and he called upon me."

The chief's eyes widened. "Let them through," he ordered the guards, who parted.

"I thought you would be fending off men from the west when I got here, but I see no fight. Why have you called for aid?"

"It is not here where we are set upon, but our hunting grounds and places where things grow," the chief said, looking Korgorun up and down in disbelief. Though tall, he was not exceptional to look at. At least baring no divine markings or godly glow. But the chief looked at him as if he bore both. "It is an honour to see you here in answer to my prayer."

"Because of your prayer, I stood in my father's presence. It is *you* who honours *me*."

"Come," the chief invited, leading them into his large tent. "I have prepared the tokroot draft for your arrival," he said, pointing to a large bowl filled with the cloudy liquid orcs imbibed for its numbing effects.

A bowl made from some animal skull, grounded smooth, was passed from orc to orc as each partook in the cloudy draft.

"The humans of the westlands have crossed the Gods

Spine and, at the base of the mountains, made a fort in our territory," the chief explained.

"How?" Korgorun asked, angered. "Are not the great passes watched and the high rocky paths patrolled?"

"They must have come in this winter just passed when there was too little to hunt and too little that grew in the lands about it. Either they came when none watched or defeated those who made to stop them. I cannot say. Only that when my tribe returned to hunt at the dawn of warmer days, the fort was there. Tall and sharpened trunks make walls where the rocks do not already. Most of the work was done by the mountain long ago. The humans are safe inside and make to patrol our lands, hunting our meat, and plucking our fruit, leaves, and roots."

Korgorun thought for a moment, wrinkling his youthful brow, and closing his eyes.

"We have dwindled our number making to breach their stronghold," the chief said. "We could move our village, but then we'd be letting the humans gain a foothold in our lands."

"I must see this fort for myself," Korgorun said. "Only then will I know what must be done."

"We can get to no place above it, and It cannot be seen from the deep paths that lead down the mountains. Not until nearly on the ground."

"Then let us go there."

Korgorun crouched behind rocks with his six followers and an additional six orcs from the mountain village. The view of the human fort from the highest place it could be seen only revealed so much. He could see the debranched trunks, tied together, and sharpened into spikes that pointed toward the sky. Guards walked some high platform behind them. Dark smoke rose from within. Korgorun hummed knowingly. "They work a fire hot, making metal from the rocks they know to look for. What the humans lack in strength they make up for in cunning and craft." Korgorun sneered, as he looked about. He noticed a small stream flowing out into the woods. "They have their own water."

"It falls and runs down the mountains above them," one of the Cru-Gol-Yr orcs said, as if knowing what Korgorun was going to ask next.

Korgorun tilted his head back, slowly looking up the mountain. "Do you know where this water comes from? A place we can reach?"

The other orc nodded. "The water that runs near our camp comes from the same place."

Korgorun smiled, rubbing his thumb over one of his tusks. "They came in the winter and felled bare trees. Now is the spring when things grow, and they have their own water. But what if it flowed no more?"

The thirteen returned to Cru-Gol-Yr and pushed northward beyond it, higher through the mountains, climbing as they followed the stream that provided water for the orcs of the village. They climbed until they found a place where three streams stemmed from a broader one, branching out into different directions. Few plants grew nearby in the rocky plateau that Korgorun looked upon as he waited for the others to catch up. Though patient for those who accompanied him, not having the tireless endurance of one who carried gods blood, he despised standing still when his mind was set on a task. And so, he began climbing one of two rocky spires that stood close together. He climbed through the gap, about twenty feet above the plateau, and wedged himself between the towers of rock, pressing his back against one and his feet against its neighbour.

As the other orcs reached the place where the stream divided thrice, they knelt and sat to catch their breath. They had climbed far and exerted themselves in keeping up with the son of a demigod. Some looked up, bracing themselves for more work.

"Rest," Korgorun called down to them. "Drink of the

water. But be wary of what may fall."

He pressed his feet hard against one rock and his hands against the other by his head. He pushed, attempting to straighten his legs as he flexed his entire body. Small rocks loosened and fell as the tall rocky spires made cracking sounds. Slivers of rock began to shave off and slide down the formation, smashing on the hard ground below. He began to growl, putting everything he had into it.

The orcs below moved themselves, shuffling away from the likely direction larger pieces might fall. Deeper cracks sounded and vibrated in the rock as he felt the formation begin to concede to his will. More pieces broke free as he felt a small shift. He began stomping one of his feet in frustration against the opposing rock. Now yelling at it in anger, "Break, damn you."

There was an echoing crack, louder than the others, and the peak of the rock came down, falling dangerously close past him. No sooner than it had smashed on the ground, half of what was left of the top third of the formation split in the middle. It too slid off, giving his foot nothing but air to kick. He twisted, and tried to bring down more, but he could not get the same purchase on the rock. At least no position that would yield as effective results. He looked down at the rubble he made and was proud. "I think that's enough," he thought aloud.

"For what?" one of his followers asked.

Korgorun climbed down and dusted his hands. "Gather all the loose rocks that may be found in this place and bring them here." He picked up one of the larger chunks of rock he had brought down and smashed it against another, breaking it into smaller fragments.

As the other orcs complied, he gripped the largest piece and dragged it to the stream. He had to labour to lift it over the northernmost branch of the stream, then wedged it into the central channel as close to the juncture as he could manage. One of his followers, gathering rocks close by, raised his brow.

"We will block the middle stream with rock and parch the fort at the foot of the mountain," Korgorun explained. "They have built upon our lands, felled our trees, slaying our animals and kin. But when their water runs dry. They will have to come out and face us when *we* are ready."

It took them some time to block the flow of the central stream and pile more rock at the juncture so that water didn't simply flow over or around to find its way to the humans. They laboured until nothing flowed past their rock dam. They dug what earth they could from where they found it and compacted it just past the rock pile.

"Now we gather every fighting orc from your tribe," he told the village orcs, "and wait in the woods."

The chief was most impressed with the tactic when they returned and told him of what they had done. They sent scouts to watch over the fort while they took the night to rest. In the morning, they passed the scouts, sending them to watch the north stream, and made for the woods where they set up camp directly east of the fort.

The humans did not surface for days, keeping Korgorun and the other orcs waiting. All grew restless and impatient, wanting to attack the fort for those who had fallen to the humans' hunting parties.

Eventually, the gate opened. Too far to rush from anywhere hidden, the orcs watched from afar. Three men were released, armed with spears, tipped by the brown metal, and swords by their sides. The same metal hung upon their bodies fixed upon treated hide. They carried with them each a pair of wooden pails. Korgorun grinned, knowing they had been sent to fetch water, being now denied by the mountain. He took with him his six followers and made the rest wait where they were.

They followed the three men from a distance who seemed at least wise enough to be constantly looking around, fearful of those whose lands they had invaded. They continued watching them as they drank from the stream, then filled their pails. They hung the filled vessels by their rope handles on their spears to carry them over their shoulders. Burdened so, they were unready for combat when it descended upon them. They dropped their tangled spears and spilled their water to draw their metal blades. Each man was at least a foot shorter than Korgorun and near as much as his companions, who had reach and number over them. Though their blades sliced orcflesh and tasted orc blood, they did not prevail.

One of the injured orcs clutched at a wound in his leg. "Their weapons cut deep, just by touch," he observed, though his wound had not crippled him.

"We should have attacked them while they were drinking," another said, whose shoulder had caught the swift wrath of a human's blade.

"I needed to see how they meant to carry the water," Korgorun explained, turning all heads towards him in curiosity. "Someone fetch the scouts," he ordered, squatting by one of the dead men. There, he found a much shorter blade upon the human's belt. A dagger. He drew it and brushed his thumb against the edge to test its sharpness. He licked his lower lip, sliding his tongue between his tusks in contemplation. He took the corpse's hand and raised it so he could compare the skin of the arm with his own. "The humans will still get their water. But much closer to nightfall."

While many tribes and clans of orc abandoned their smaller infants at birth, there were those who had the foresight to use them as scouts. Their runted size made them light on their feet, good at hiding, and in this case, a comparable size to the humans of the fort. As the insects of the forest began to make their evening noises, three scouts were chosen to wear the dead men's armour, their weapons, and their scalped curly black hair was placed on their own bald green heads. The spears were placed over their shoulders to balance the water pails the way the humans had done.

"Remember, you will only seem like the humans to those on the walls," Korgorun said. "Once the gate is open, they will see what you are. Kill those at the gate. Take the crossbar or log that locks the gate and toss it out of the fort so that it cannot be locked shut again. Stay near the gate until we can reach you." He saw fear in the eyes. Though they'd never admit to it, they were right to feel it. There was much uncertainty in what they must do. But they were brave enough to agree to such a dangerous task, and that filled Korgorun's heart with pride.

"We do not speak the human tongue," one scout said. "What should we do if they call to us as we approach?"

"The humans have many tongues with many words. Divided more than most who walk the earth. I cannot teach you words of whichever they speak. So, just mumble back. They'll have to open the gate just to hear you." He patted the scout on the shoulder, who laughed. "Just remember to take what cover you may when the gate is open. We will run to you, and I will be the first to follow you through the gates. Then we will fight together. Side by side."

When the scouts carried the water to the gate from the north, those upon the walls called down to them, asking where they had been. With the blood of gods in his veins, Korgorun understood them. He did not know the words, but he always knew the meaning. The scouts shrugged in their disguises, keeping the faces low as they spoke subdued gibberish that sounded to orc ears like the human speak.

The call to open the gate echoed as Korgorun and those with him poised ready to sprint from behind rocks and trees. When the gate opened, it was not opened far before the humans saw the truth. They made to push it shut again, forcing the disguised orcs to barge back against the gate.

Korgorun began running as fast as he could as those behind him attempted to keep up.

The battle for the gate heaved back and forth, as more humans piled on the inside to shut it again. There was yelling from the wall about the gate and soon about the small horde charging towards them. Korgorun's unnatural speed and strength widened the gap between him and those following behind. He leapt high, knocking the gate open as he pounded it shoulder-first, throwing his whole body at it. Those trying to shut it were knocked to the ground as he rolled in past the scouts. He continued in, getting back to his feet, and running for the nearest ladder that led to the bulwark.

The scouts in human armour slew the men on the ground by the gate and dragged the crossbar from the gate, tossing it out as the other orcs approached. All eyes inside were on Korgorun, bounding the stairs as he drew his stone axe. Those on the narrow walkway ran at him with spears, tipped with the brown metal. He hurled his axe at the first man so hard that it bent the metal he wore on his chest when it struck him. With his hands free, Korgorun caught the upper shafts of the spears and pushed the men back into those behind them. He let the shafts slide through his hands and crossed them, forcing one man off the edge and the other over the wall, out of the fort.

The other orcs came charging through the open gate and spread wide. They caught a line of men off-guard who were running for the stairs to face Korgorun.

Korgorun collected his axe from the coughing man on his back, not cut by the axe, but crushed by it. He then ploughed through the rest of the defences while the orcs on the ground fought the men defending their fort. As the men in their armour ran towards Korgorun with their metal blades raised and ready, he let out a mighty shout that tore through the air and shook splinters from the wood and dust from the rocks, all blasting at those in the wake of his voice. Several fell, blinded by the debris. Those who didn't were knocked off the walkway by the shaft of Korgorun's axe.

Soon the battle was over, with all humans either dead or injured. Those who survived were stripped naked and bound. Their weapons and armour piled together.

"This fort now belongs to the orcs of Cru-Gol-Yr," Korgorun announced. "These soldiers will be your slaves until they can serve you no more. Their metal will serve…" The orcs all suddenly fell to one knee in reverence. "No. Do not bow to me, I am not your-"

"They do not bow to you," a voice said beside him.

Startled, he made to raise his axe, but a stronger hand stayed him as he turned to see Ochius, his father. There before, all in the waking world.

"Must you make to strike me every time?" He asked, amused. Korgorun fell also to his knee. "You have served me and your fellow orcs well, my son." He snatched the stone axe and tossed it to the ground below. "That is not a weapon befitting one who carries my blood. This is." He held up another axe. It wasn't as large as the stone one, made for a single hand, but its blade was made from the same purple metal as the knives at Ochius's side. The blade was made of straight edges, crafted with intention and skill.

"I am honoured to receive it, father," Korgorun said.

"There might be one for your other hand, one day, if you continue to serve me well."

Korgorun bowed his head again.

"This stronghold is a good prize, but it could use some water flowing into it," Ochius said with an amused hum.

When Korgorun looked back up, his father was gone. He looked to the orcs still kneeling on the ground, but they had kept their heads low in reverence. All that remained was an axe made of a metal from another realm. As he stood, he looked to the mountains, knowing he had to climb them again to free the stream he had dammed.

He gathered his followers and left the orcs to hold their new fort as they praised him and his father for sending him.

49

He left his large stone axe at the fort so that one amongst the orcs there could wield it, boasting that it was given by Korgorun, son of Ochius.

GRANDCHILDREN OF GOD

B.F. VEGA

Bodil looked out onto a troubled sea. The wind blew her long blond curls into her eyes. She held aloft the sun stone and then shouted orders to her helmsman before jumping down and taking up an oar herself. Gregor looked at his sister who was now chief of their tribe since the death of their father. As a grand-daughter of Ragnor Lothbrook, she had a claim to her grandfather's kingdom if she could convince her many cousins and uncles to accept her rule. Gregor was happy to help her. They had been born but 12 minutes apart, and he knew that the only allegiance either could count on in this harsh world was from each other.

They sailed the North Sea toward the colony of Iceland. Lankan of the Northern Ice had spoken out against a mere woman leading his people. Not only was she a mere woman, but a Christian convert at that. Gregor pitied Lankan. His sister was the fiercest fighter Gregor had ever seen.

He looked down at the scroll in front of him. One of the great advantages he and his sister had over Jarls like Lankan was that they had been taught to read and write. This dispatch was interesting, and he did not really know what to think about it. Lankan claimed that Loki himself, in the shape of a giant serpent, had appeared in the lava and ice fields near Lankans village and that with the true Norse gods on their side they could easily defeat the little Christian girl.

Even if Gregor had not been a convert to the new God, he would have doubted the story. Lankan's clan had never been influential or powerful. If one of the old gods was invoking a rebellion, why would it choose Lankan?

Gregor reached up to the dual pendants that he wore. One in the shape of a cross and the other a hammer. It was said that no matter how devout a Northerner was to Christ while on land, when on the stormy Northern Sea they all belonged to Thor. Gregor always felt conflicted about this, but in the 10 years he and his sister had been sailing he had seen things that made no sense unless there were forces at work beyond what the monks told.

They were approaching the Orkney Islands where they would stop, and resupply. As they approached the island that held their destination The Village of the Figs, he saw that they had arrived just in time. The sky ahead of them was turning black and sheets of rain were already falling on the seas. Their boats were very seaworthy, but the thin hulls and lack of any cover made them freezing and miserable during storms.

Even with Bodil's near mythical navigating and the men rowing their hardest the storm hit them before they had reached the harbor, leaving them soaked to the skin by the time they had beached the boat and sludged up the path to the Jarls hall. Bodil led the way, but suddenly stopped just outside of the circle of houses that made up the small settlement. She pulled her axe free and gave the signal for caution.

Gregor could not see what she saw at first. But then he saw two Ravens fly up and perch on the peaked roof of the longhouse. One of them held in its beak a long bloody string that ended in a human eye.

Bodil gestured to her men to start searching the homes. The troop of 70 men that had been in the boat with her and

Gregor fanned out as Bodil waited for Gregor to come up to her.

They did not need to speak. He knew the eye meant death had come. He also knew that the Ravens would be taken as an omen that Odin himself stood against them, unless Bodil and Gregor could prove otherwise.

They walked forward down the empty street and entered the longhouse. Gregor had taken part in many bloody and horrific battles, but the sight that met his eyes when he walked into the longhouse was horrific even by Northern standards. The entire longhouse was coated in blood. It looked like the entire village — women, children, men, and animals had been slaughtered. The bodies had been mutilated and he could tell that some of them had been mutilated before death had finally taken them. They picked their way past the desecrated stinking corpses. They had swelled little so they could not have been more than a day dead. Careful so as not to draw attention if the killers were still around they made their way to the Jarls seat and found what they had been dreading. The Jarl, their father's brother, was dead as well. His intestines had been nailed to his seat of power and it looked as if he had then been pulled so that they were straight and then circled back toward the throne until he was fully wrapped in his own entrails.

As they approached the body, Gregor heard the men enter the hall behind them and stand silent. He looked to his sister for her to give the order to start burying the dead, but she did not. She looked puzzled, if anything. She walked forward and placed a hand under her uncle's head, lifting it up. One of his eyes was missing and Gregor knew what was puzzling Bodil. How did the Ravens get into the sealed Longhouse and why had they only removed the eye from one of the corpses? He turned to look at the other corpses nearest him. While they were bloated, they did not have rats or bugs swarming them like they should if they had been dead longer than an hour. Something was very wrong. He approached the body of his young cousin. A boy about 8 years of age. Like the others, his stomach had been split and his intestines spilled.

Gregor got closer to the boy's body to see if he could discern why the body was not being eaten. As he did so, he finally heard his sister speak.

"Gregor no!" she yelled

Gregor turned to look at her and then turned back to see his cousin's eyes open. They were deep red, with irises as black as a starless night. The boy moved and tried to bite Gregor who jumped out of the way and looked around in horror. All the bodies were moving. Wriggling and trying to stand. Those who made it to their feet now fell on Bodil's men whose axes did not seem to have any effect in stopping the things.

"Draugr! Swing for their heads!" Bodil yelled as she brought her axe crashing down into her uncle's skull. Gregor saw the skull split open and then he watched as something long dark and the color of dying embers hauled itself out of the open wound.

He looked around to see that all the dead who had their heads split open were similarly being vacated by the things. Bodil's men had no idea how to fight these things. If you swung an axe at one, the thing would split apart like smoke and then reform. But when the things swung their long sharp claws at the men they tore flesh and ripped off noses, lips, eyes, and ears.

Gregor pulled his axe out and had started cutting off the legs of the walking dead. This led to them pulling themselves along the ground, so he started cutting off arms. At least if their heads were intact, whatever spirits were animating them seemed trapped in the bodies.

Bodil followed suit, but there were too many dead, and too many of the beasts inside of them had been released. The warriors were being literally pulled apart a chunk of flesh at a time.

Bodil looked at her brother. He nodded. If they were to die, they would do so together. They both took a step forward when the large double doors of the longhouse flung open.

A woman stood in the doorway and behind her were 100 men each taller than any of the Northmen and the Northmen were the tallest humans on the planet. The woman stepped inside and said in a booming voice, "I am Nikkal of Canaan and you will return to the depths that you have come from!"

As she said this, all the smoke creatures headed toward her direction. All the dead that could still move also turned toward her, but they never got close to her. The tall men encircled her and pulled out swords coated in something that looked like dried blood. Whenever one of the monsters touched the swords, they shriveled like fire when water was poured on it. The tall men placed their large hands on the heads of those still moving, crushing their skulls and then slaying the demons attempting to escape.

When the last demon was gone and the last dead was still, the tall men stood back from the woman who stepped forward into the grotesque scene and held out her arms.

"Bodil, Gregor. I have missed you."

Both warriors dropped their weapons and ran forward to embrace their mother.

Later, after the dead had been buried and the warriors that

had survived were ensconced in one of the vacant houses with some of Nikkal's men looking after them, the family sat around a small fire in the longhouse.

"Where have you been?" Gregor asked.

"I went to get reinforcements." She said, "I knew with your father's death that the forces that stood against me would try to take you."

"It took you 5 years to find reinforcements?" Gregor asked incredulously, looking at his sister. But she was looking at their mother in a way he had never seen her look.

"We are not Canaanites. We are of the North." Bodil said.

"Yes," their mother answered evasively.

"This island is named for a fruit that the people on it have never seen. We ourselves only found what it was when we made a pilgrimage to Constantinople with the King of the Rus." Bodil continued.

"What are you asking, daughter?" Nikkal asked

"What is the true nature of this place? And why are the Nephilim here?"

"The Nephilim?" Gregor asked

"The Nephilim were in the earth in those days, and also after that when the sons of God came in unto the daughters of men, and they bore children to them," Bodil quoted and Gregor recognized the passage from The Book of Genesis.

"The men?" Gregor asked

"Yes, Sons of Canaanite women and the angels of God." Bodil answered, "Isn't that right Nikkal of Canaan?"

Nikkal looked at her two children before answering. "I was a widow, heavy with child at the time I met the man you knew as your father. Your true father was killed by his own brother. I could have no more children after you two. Mortal bodies are not meant to bear the children of God, so your father took you two as his own. But he knew what you were and agreed that you should be taught everything you could before your uncles learned of your existence. These men with me, these Nephilim were the forefathers of all the Northmen. When they were forced from Canaan, the survivors came north and from the children of these men all Northerners were born. I and my husband were still safe in a small orchard protected from the wrath of his vengeful and jealous brethren at the time. When he was killed, I came to join those who were like the children I was about to bear. You two were the last to be born of a mortal woman and the host of god."

"This is blasphemy," Gregor said

"Be still." Bodil answered him, "Tell me, mother. Who stands against us? Surely, Lankan does not have the power to raise Draugr?"

"No. The creatures you encountered in the longhouse today come from your uncle's realm. Your men know him as Loki the trickster, the serpent. I knew him as Lucifer the father of lies, the beautiful morning star. He seeks to cause havoc because he can. He hates both the children of God and the children of man. But most of all he hates Gabriel who had him cast from Heaven. It is Gabriel, who stands against you. Lucifer/Loki is merely using you as bait."

"What now?" Bodil asked

"Now, you sleep. Tomorrow, you two lead my men to continue your journey to the barren field of ice and fire beyond Lankan's village. Lucifer has chosen his location well. With all the Nephilim there, Gabriel will not be able to resist it, and no humans will witness the fractured truth of Heaven."

"And then?" Gregor asked

"And then?" Nikkal laughed, "Children, from Byzantium to Vinland they refer to you as the Alpha and the Omega of the Sea Wolves. Then you fight. You restore your father's honor, and you rid this world of the horrors you saw today."

The next morning as Bodil and Gregor went to join the other Nephilim on the boat Nikkal came up to them. She handed Bodil a sheathed sword saying, "I know that you prefer your war-axe, but this was your father's sword."

Bodil unsheathed the blade, and it glinted golden in the sunlight. Nikkal then handed Gregor a bow and quiver like the one he was taught to use in Constantinople, saying, "Sometimes, the best tactic is to not be within striking range."

She hugged her children, and they turned to leave. But Gregor turned back and asked, "Who was our true father?"

Nikkal answered, "His name was Shamyaza, and you wear his emblem with your cross."

The crossing to Iceland was rough. They beached that night in the small port of Reykjavik and were met by Olaf, Lankan's eldest son, and a dozen unarmed villagers running toward their boat.

Gregor grabbed Olaf. "What is the matter, man? Where is your father?"

"Dead." Olaf said his face was as gray as dried lava on snow. "And walking," Olaf screamed, pointing to where he and the townsfolk with him had just come from and, in the weakest point of the torches they could see Lankan. His stomach was ripped open, his intestines spilled with every faltering step.

Bodil motioned the Nephilim forward. She turned to Gregor, "Stay here, guard Olaf and the villagers. We will need information to press forward."

Gregor nodded and readied his bow in case any of the Draugr got past Bodils warriors.

Bodil and her men entered the settlement, hacking through Draugr as they went. The fighting here was harder than at the longhouse. The smoke demons seemed stronger, and it took more blows to disperse them. These could also use mortal weapons, making them much more dangerous than the others of their kind. Bodil turned to her mother's second in command and asked, "Why are these more powerful?"

"The closer we draw to their master. The more power he can endow them with." The Nephilim answered.

Bodil nodded that made sense to her. "Crush all the walking dead then withdraw away from the village toward the beach," she ordered. Her men did so and the smoke demons now all freed from the dead followed them. The farther from the village they got the weaker the demons became, first dropping mortal weapons, then being easier to kill. By the time the last had been defeated Bodil and her men were standing in waist deep water with no further point to withdraw to.

Returning to Gregor she informed the villagers that their settlement was safe for the moment. She then turned to Olaf.

"Tell me."

"Yesterday, the great serpent was spotted outside of town again. My father thought to bargain with it to make him more powerful than the little Christian girl...His words not mine!" Olaf whimpered.

"You have not one ounce of your father's spirit." Gregor said in disgust.

"My father did not return until daybreak. Two of his men carried him in a litter. His stomach had been ripped open by the great serpent's tooth. Most of his men had been lost. He died soon after reaching the longhouse. At sunset, he rose from his bed and attacked my mother as she attempted to prepare his body for burial. Then more of his men came into town. You saw them, some of them had just fragments of flesh holding on hands or heads. But they quickly overpowered the warriors in town. The newly dead also rose and joined my father and his men."

"How did you come to not be attacked in the onslaught?" Gregor asked.

"I was with my mistress. I was protecting her by hiding her under the bed until we were able to make our escape to the beach."

Bodil looked at the handful of villagers that had survived, "Which is your mistress?" She asked.

"She did not make it." Olaf said without meeting their

gaze.

"You mean you sacrificed her to save yourself?" Gregor said and looked at his sister who was fingering her sword. He shook his head and turned to the villagers saying, "Behold Olaf the spineless. Spread his infamy."

"What! No!" Olaf wailed.

"Prove us wrong. Show us where the snake is." Gregor answered him.

Olaf looked as if he wanted to cry, but as the villagers snickered behind him he pulled himself up straight and said to Bodil, in a voice not overly shaky, "This way Milady."

Bodil poked him with her sword and he yelped, before leading them away from the beach and back through the town.

They headed north out of the small settlement, following a path of blood and bile that had come from the shuffling undead. Soon they crested a ridge that allowed them to look down into a land that was ice and fire as far as they could see. In the middle of this vast field was a single tree where no tree should have been able to grow. Coiled around the tree was a great serpent.

"Jormungand" Olaf breathed.

"Lucifer" Gregor and Bodil said

They heard a great laughter coming from the serpent at it

slithered toward them slowly morphing into a man as it went.

"Oh, my nieces and nephews. I have been waiting for so long." It said.

"What do you want of us?" Bodil asked

"Merely vengeance on my brother, Gabriel." The serpent man answered.

"What do we have to do with that?" Gregor asked

"Ah, well, you see, to kill an angel takes the blood of another angel. I'm not exactly welcome in heaven anymore, and I'm rather fond of my own blood. Lucky for me, that all of you have enough angelic blood to make it work." He then winked at Bodil, pulled a dagger and lunged.

Bodil pushed Olaf in front of her, using his soft body as a shield as she and the Nephilim encircled the man with weapons drawn.

Lucifer dropped Olaf's lifeless body and wiped the dagger off on his leg.

"I had to try," he laughed. Bodil was about to respond when a sound like a great trumpet was heard echoing around the valley.

"Ah, right on time!" Lucifer sneered and then shifted back into snake form, quickly disappeared into a great crack in the ground.

A pure white light was bathing the field, and it slowly coalesced into a legion of men. At the front of them, holding a sword in one hand and a trumpet in the other was the archangel Gabriel. He looked at the gathered Nephilim and sneered at them. "Abominations."

Bodil sliced her own palm and anointing her sword she ran toward the host. Where the blood on her blade touched the angelic skin, it sizzled and split. She knew that she was going to need more blood. She cut her other palm as well and coated the blade enough to make a clean swipe through an angel's neck. When the body fell, she sheathed her sword in the neck cavity and used the now blood covered blade to take down the next host. Her army followed suit.

Her hands ached and bled on the pommel, making it slippery, but she was given no time to dwell on that. The Nephilim were the fiercest fighters the earth had ever seen, but they fought a far older, far more powerful enemy. She headed straight toward the tree, taking down any who got in her way.

As she reached the tree, Gabriel himself suddenly appeared beside her and only a quick move on her part saved her arm from his blade. He stumbled a bit, and she placed her bloody palm on the tree of life, saying, "Father. We need you."

A great thunderclap was heard, and then lightning rained down onto the battlefield. Gregor pulled his bloodied axe from an angel's neck and watched as lightning bolts shaped like hammers struck the host.

Then Gabriel raised his sword and hacked through the bough that Bodil's blood covered. As it fell away, the sky cleared.

"You are clever like your mother. But not clever enough." He said to her.

Bodil did not bother to engage in conversation. She struck at Gabriel's sword.

Gregor could see the Nephilim being cut down. He knew they were losing. He looked up to see a circle of host starting to enclose his sister. She now battled a dozen angels and Gabriel himself. Gregor started dipping arrows in the blood around him and took down angel after angel as they went to strike Bodil. Soon, only Gabriel was left, but there was no more fresh blood. He didn't think twice. His sister was in danger. He drew his dagger and opened the large vein that ran down his leg. With the last of his strength, he dipped his arrow into his own blood and shot. The arrow struck true, protruding from Gabriel's breast. The skin around it sizzled and started to rot. Bodil knew what this meant. She quickly pushed past the injured angel and ran toward the direction the arrow had come from.

She was too late to do anything but hold her brother as the last of his blood left his open veins.

"Avenge us." He whispered as his eyes glossed over and his breath ceased.

Bodil stood and turned. The Nephilim were few and far between. Gabriel was on the ground and hosts were trying to pull the arrow from his breast. They may lose this day, but Gabriel would pay for her brother's death. She anointed her sword with Gregor's blood and the blood still oozing from her own hand. She then ran straight to the fallen arch-angel. She pushed past the others, ignoring arrows and sword wounds. She got to the fallen host and with a mighty battle cry cut his head from his body. Then she pulled his head from the ground and drank the blood coming from it, holding it in her mouth to spit onto the blade as she needed it. She felt no pain, no fear, she only felt the need to send others to accompany her brother.

Finally, the last angel fell, and then her wounds took their toll. She limped back to her brother's body, allowing any of the blood still in her mouth to drop onto the ground.

She knew she was dying. She knew that she and the Nephilim were now a lost kind. But not even the host of Heaven could resurrect the dead arch-angel that had taken so much from her family, so she closed her eyes to rest.

THAT WHICH I CANNOT BUT MUST CONFESS

JORDAN DAVIDSON

VI.

I listened to you, Ash, when you said sinners are beautiful because they transcend the laws of God._ "We're deeper, Basil, deeper than those who bend in devotion, blinded by terror for their immortal souls."_ But you never taught me that we also live in fear. We have no immortal souls at all. No Torah, Talmud, Bible, or Quran. Only this courtroom, with wood paneled walls and prosecuting attorneys baptizing their tongues with paper cups. Reporters and camera men. You. Me. Sinners, all of us.

I'm watching the fluorescent lights wash over your skin and counting how many of us are left. You're here. You dodge questions like bullets with your old, sultry grin. I'm here. Madon sits outside and makes small talk with plaintiffs, tucking their diamond rings in his tuxedo pockets. Luci glows on television above him, where she preaches to millions of people that they must turn their faces to people like Tanya...Tanya herself's in jail, been there for a while. Belphry couldn't—or wouldn't—come. Lev abandoned us years ago.

A nice collection, an immortal set. Picture the lineage of the devil like a queen's inheritance. When Satan dies, another Wrath crawls from between a mother's legs. We've all been through our iterations. Only you've persisted since the fall, one unchanging line of Lust.

There is no such thing as saints, you knew. And I'll expect that to be true, even after your trial and the jury saying: Guilty. Guilty. Guilty. Guilty. Guilty. Guilty. Guilty. Guilty. Guilty. Guilty. Guilty. Guilty.

I will wonder if they sing your doom or mine.

***

III.

When the girl screamed and for the first time you couldn't

run fast enough, you came to my door, hands covered in blood, unrepentant, unconcerned, unholy, and unforgiving. I should have shut the door and glued the windows, blocked the chimney, called the police. But before I could, before I even thought about saying no, I had given you a towel and asked what had happened, not what you'd done.

When you stepped in, the windows were open. Clean. You called my house so clean. I never cared for sparkling counters, but I kept cat hair off the curtains and dusted the bookshelves. Buried underneath cheap romance novels and crumpled grocery coupons lay my bound Torah copy. You picked it up. Threw it across the room.

"Still reading it?" You asked.

Not sure of what to do, I leaned against the wall with exhaustion. "And you don't?"

"Burned it. End of the first century."

"Before you knew what we were."

"Before you'd been born, Love."

My teeth slipped on my tongue. The coppery taste always helped satisfy the cravings. "What do you need, Ash?"

You smiled at me, brilliant and perfect, one bloody hand extended towards me with wiggling fingers. Each one of your teeth outshone a pearl. Each one of your eyes out burned a wildfire. "Can you kill someone, Bee?"

"Basil."

"That's a boy's name."

"Basil." You never said it right. Well, you knew like I did that Basil wasn't my name, but you had watched me as I shed the Hungarian for Beezlebub and left that one too.

"Can you kill someone?"

"Ask Tanya."

Dust flew as you fiddled with one of my figurines, a set of angel wings carved in redwood. "Tanya'd do in me instead of killing whoever I wanted dead. You know that, Love."

"Who was it this time?" I had an idea of your tastes. Already she blossomed in the folds of my mind, some blond girl, most likely cursed with wide blue eyes and sensual curves over a flat stomach. I knew what kind of beast you were. As a kid, I used to worry that you'd see my breasts and hunger for the rose between my legs, but by then I'd discovered my major flaw: you liked mortal girls. Erasable girls. "Where is she?"

"Fourth and Colfax." You responded.

"I'll call the police, get rid of your DNA. But I'm not killing her, Ash."

Smiling at me like it was such an easy request, you kissed my cheek and asked me one last thing. "And the rape kit?

Burn it, will you?"

"I will."

You held up my Torah in one hand. "You don't need this, Bee. We're infernal." Then your red hair and wildfire eyes slunk back to hide where cocaine and cigarette smoke made love to the music of gyrating flesh and sweaty palms. Their love children were the darkest shadows I'd ever met.

I, the stupid little girl, did what you asked. Later that night, I tried to drown you out with pints of ice cream, softened to slide easily down my throat. The next thirty minutes I spent curled over the toilet retching and chasing away the smell of vomit with cinnamon gum.

***

I.

I grew up in Budapest, in the Jewish quarter along the banks of the Danube. For ten years, I was born into humanity, but World War II raged; hatred brought you to me. I was ten years old the first night I saw you. The lights of the Danube christened you some holy creature; the crackling of the fire named you otherwise. You held hands with Luci; Tanya and Madon followed, laughing. Always laughing. I can't picture you in a moment when you weren't.

The Nazis were burning synagogues in the Jewish quarter. I trailed them home. No one managed to pick out a skeletal girl from the shadows, one whose food expelled itself from her mouth just minutes after it went down. I froze at the walls. Flames devoured what remained of my home— no doubt I would scorch my fingers to the bone digging through the still sparking cremation of all that I knew. Mesmerized by the grotesque and choked by the helplessness, I buried myself in the shadows of the walls, assuming that when those men in hate-woven uniforms found me, I'd meet the same fate as my sisters. As the firelight distorted their faces, I memorized the countenances of true demons.

And I scrambled to fling myself onto the pyre.

But you stepped forward. Your hands whirled matches like eleven tiny magic wands. "Are you going to come out and help us, little sinner?"

In the second between heartbeats that it took for it to dawn on me that your words weren't for the abominations of men that stood before us, my whole body tightened into a loaded pistol.

"A dud." Tanya readied her automatic.

Luci produced a knife from the crimson folds of her gown. "And I thought she'd be one of us nearly worth my time."

You smiled. The wildfire in your eyes raged in your

tastebuds, popping like unopened soda cans, fire in the lines of your palms, which people rumored to tell the future. "Devour them, love."

For so long, I had waged war on my hunger. It would seize a fort; I would gulp a scrap of bread. But it would always gain again to send me rifling through the dirt for something, anything, to eat. And later, in my shame, when the urges infiltrated me again to continue eating? I pulled God given reflexes with fingers down my throat.

The hunger took me. Blue eyes cut down the skeletal girl stepping from the shadows. But I bit back.

When the Nazis died, I didn't leave a cell of them left. Their essence was mine, absorbed through the outrage in my skin, dismantled through the hatred in my tongue.

I finished the magic show weeping. You took my hands, which had begun to shake.

"Well done." You said.

Well done.

***

II.

I followed you to America. You loved this country for its freedom and for what nefarious actions that freedom propelled when social consequence failed. _"With choice"_ —you told me— _"comes our inherent evil"_. And in this vacuum, I learned of your trade, of my own immortality.

1950, and Madon and I met at a rundown tavern in Virginia to discuss the most intriguing future: The Cold War. The bar reeked of warm beer and half bleached wooden benches still absorbing the last traces of the previous night's drunkards and champions. Madon poured me a glass and began the business of laying out temptation. "A senator. Joseph McCarthy," he said. "The guy's already overcome by Luci's syndrome, and I'm working my magic. All we need is you."

I pushed the drink away. The day-old taste of my sins and bar peanuts didn't mix well with scotch. "Why?"

With an exhale that spoke of further business postponed by a child's explanation, Madon set down his money clip, letting the smooth roll of Benjamin Franklins cascade over his fingers in a tidal wave of hypnotic motion. "Luci's got his pride going. Pride—" Madon broke off in laughter, "for this little thing she calls a country. Nationalism. Enough to make an honest man go crazy. She's going to show 'em commies." His disbelief at Luci's frivolity made his words long and languid, lazy summer days.

"And you'll let her?" Memories of Hungary still had me screaming, pacing the room with fire in my feet.

"Start a manhunt for communists? Why not? Better for my business isn't it?"

I hated every word he said. I hated his thirst for money, his casual consumption. But we hate the bits of ourselves we find in other people, don't we?

Madon gave me time to think and let me walk home early. As I finished my grocery runs and polished waxy apples with my sleeve, I lifted the rotary phone to call you, still getting used to dialing. It took me four tries to ring you in. "Ash—"

You picked up on the second ring. "You can still come over now, I've got another girl here but..." Sensuality sent my stomach going; the loaf of bread I'd just bought began to disappear in large chunks. Crumbs decorated my upper lip.

"Ash."

"Basil." Disappointment. That was disappointment ringing through the line. _You always liked erasable girls._

Keys clattered to the floor; I struggled to unlock the pantry door. In the space of time it had taken me to bend down and snatch them up again, I heard nothing but silence. A pause, stretched out through the centuries, and finally: "What do you want?"

"Advice."

"If it's about eating, Basil, I'm not one to tell you what to do. Tanya's still in prison, so if you want someone to kick your ass, stage a riot."

"It's not about that." I took a bag of chocolates from the shelf, unwrapped them, and ate them one by one, letting each molecule melt to the back of my throat. "Madon wants me to..."

You let loose a strangled chuckle. "You're calling me in the middle of," In the background, a bed creaked and someone groaned, " — to ask me about Madon?"

"There's a senator. He wants...Madon wants my help to get McCarthy to drink. Eat butter too, whole sticks. Madon says Luci's already in on it, getting the whole country fired up about Russia and China and the like, and the senator they've picked has no qualms about throwing a few people under the bus to climb up out of a flyover state."

"It's your job, Basil. The government wants to restrict ideas? Let them. It's not your business to stop it."

"But it is my business to help?"

"Exactly my point, love. I'll do my work, you do yours. And put the Torah away, won't you? That's not who you are anymore."

My tongue became leaden in my mouth. You disconnected the line. I remembered your eyes: wildfire. I remembered the synagogue: hate fire. I remembered Madon's voice: the fire of ambition. This time the numbers came smoothly like I was leaving my body and entering yours; you would never let a fellow sinner stand alone.

250 names. Joseph McCarthy told the American people that he knew of 250 officials leaking secrets to the communists. Luci and Madon threw a party to celebrate. Over glasses of champagne, I watched my own eyes in the mirror, remembering when I'd thought the Nazis were veritable demons. I couldn't distinguish my face from theirs—at your request, I had done the unthinkable. When McCarthy marched American citizens to jail for suspected ideologies, I only saw my family and I marching to the ghettos.

Luci crowed. Madon congratulated. I followed the Hollywood ten and wished I had the strength to remain silent. You assured me I was right to do it. And I believed you because you saved me...because you showed me...because I was too weak to...because in my head I still loved you...because I couldn't break away. Because you had been my salvation, and I owed you more loyalty than I owned myself.

***

IV.

So after your midnight rapes, I hid the girls. Called the hospitals. Buried police records and built a mausoleum of my morals, still and untouchable in death.

You never doubted me.

I put every effort into never doubting you.

V.

Sixty years after I had stopped aging, I met Mika Mercourt in Central Park. She was the most beautiful creature I'd ever been with, untouched in her faith, stormy in her darkness, and infinitely fallible. She visited my house, often enough for you to notice. I saw her, and I loved her. You saw her, and you took her. I brought flowers to her grave. Suicide, the coroners said. Suicide after rape. They couldn't very well print that the cause of her death had been a doomed immortal—you.

Slowly, like the saltwater drying on my face, I drifted away from you. Found a new city. Read and reread my Torah, hoping to find in it salvation. You and I both kept books. Yours was a trophy book, bits of hair and clothing from late-night conquests and roofies. My was newspaper clippings and fast food labels—your pride, mine shame. Every night I stood in the shower shrieking, begging the hot water to scald away your touch, your voice. I felt each time your fingers had rested on my skin; every print left an oil scar. But the marks stretched deeper than the surface cells.

For all those years I had hidden you, for all those years I had sheltered you and let you do your worst without batting my eyes. I was just as guilty as you.

And the doorbell rang. Two years since I'd seen you last, and yet my fingers turned off the water and toweled off my hair without permission. The same fingers dressed me, reached for a phone, then pulled back. You stood by the door, calmly as the day you first came, once again dripping in blood.

"One more time, Bee?" I knew that voice. I knew what you had done.

"I'll call the coroner." The kitchen walls inched closer. Lines blurred in my eyes, pixilated messages rushed back through clear glass. 911. 911. 911.

I don't remember you running when they came. I like to think that maybe the weight started to pull you down. But they wouldn't catch you, wouldn't charge you for every single girl. They couldn't track the centuries, the eons. And in my shame, I knew I'd helped you. The blood on your hands only coated mine all the more thoroughly because I'd known, and I'd let you. The two hundred and fifty-one girls you'd taken? They were my victims too.

***

VII.

Police brought you to the courtroom. I stood in the back, prosecutors whispering illegal advice into my ears, and now I watch you—unrepentant you, with unease prickling your face like you know I've doomed not just you but me, and I'm thinking to myself: _Child of my heart and child of God. The sum of our sins or more parts than can be seen of us from opening eyes. Oh God, I have created. Oh God, what have I done? They smile. Cold teeth, white collars of priests and yamukas of rabbis to tell me that this sin does not follow my skin and coat me with infernal sweat. Is this true hell?_

I can't meet your eyes over the roar of the courtroom. I'm dying, blue and frozen in the reporters's lights. You challenge me. Dare me. Know me. I am nothing more than the skin I'm in and the skin you've given me, covered in oil stains.

And I'm thinking of the silent in Hollywood and the girls who take after me and can't hold down a meal and you who I've done nothing but help. _Who are the real sinners? What are their sins?_

I am the real sinner. 72 years of it, all with a youthful face.

And the judge says _all rise_ to hold us to a moral standard, but we don't have any morality. You said I was a sinner and God had made me a sinner, but how he's made my heart and hands isn't for you to decide. You called. I held. You ran. I held. And I'm thinking: _Sinners. Ash. Sinner. Luci. Sinner. Madon. Sinner. Tanya. Sinner. Lev. Sinner. Belphry. Sinner.

Basil.

Sinner._

We stand, and I swear my soul to God and truth. My hands gorge lines of fabric from the witness stand, just as I want to do the same: gorge until I feel every molecule slide down my throat, until I'm sick and choke while bending over a marble toilet bowl cleaned using the dollars of taxes I can't pay because I don't own anything—not even myself.

You meet me at the stand. I taste the fear in your eyes. It's the same as the fear in my mouth. But I do it. I force my tongue to move.

Guilty. Guilty. Guilty. Guilty. Guilty. Guilty. Guilty. Guilty. Guilty. Guilty. Guilty. Guilty.

They ring in your doom.

And willingly, I ring in mine.

RISKY RENDEZVOUS

SULTANA RAZA

Part One

Bairoop came every year on the day when he'd first laid sight on her. A fit man in his forties, with a few wisps of grey fringing his browned face, which crow's feet had brushed very sparingly. He stared with vivid grey eyes. No, this rose-colored bust didn't do her justice, but it was all he had left. Except for a gold locket whose edges had become frayed by his fingers caressing it too much.

The tall, imposing man had to make sure he wore non-descript black clothes whose modernity he secretly despised, and kept circulating, staying out of the guards' radars.

Yet, it was a ritual Bairoop couldn't resist. He had to tear himself away before the guards were forced to usher him out. Why did she have to die so many millennia before her time?

***

Why did Saimara have to be imprisoned in that cold, grey hall, with so many strangers? Bairoop had thought of spiriting her away. But no. She was safe enough here.

Why do anything that would bring official attention to himself? An unknown man, living on the edges of polite society; an vagrant, a misfit, an eccentric, who never stayed for too long on any land; on any continent, even.

But still, every year Bairoop risked getting checked, having his false papers discovered, his identity revealed to be fake by those inhuman infernal machines of theirs.

Risked getting nabbed by pseudo-scientists like his guard Taifa. Risked getting interred in some underground state facility. Risked having his insides slashed open like his personal guard Thushra. To be examined by robotic surgeons with icy eyes. Risked being put into hypnotic trances by potent potions like his secretary Karamat. Risked having his memories probed, prodded by inhumane psychiatrists like cook Fitura. All his faithful team who'd been taken by these new mortals one by one. He'd managed to free them all, but they'd been obliged to go underground after their release. Somehow, he'd remained free all these decades. He risked being forced to disclose the exact whereabouts of his treasure trove undisturbed for a few millennia.

For what was the use of jewels when she wasn't there to be dressed in it?

Yet, he showed up, year after year, to keep her company on that special day. The only day that mattered to him. The only reason he kept count of their now defunct calendar. At least his ancient calendar differed from the modern calendar, so he came on a different day every year. The day their names had been joined in a sacred union before their whole world, as they knew it then.

He couldn't risk leaving any flowers before her bust inside the dratted museum. Yet, he made sure a new flower was laid, hidden amongst the hyacinth bushes in the green patch outside the monstrous grey building that caged her along with a papyrus card inscribed with her name in very ancient hieroglyphs that no mortal could decipher now.

This was the only way left to him to communicate silently with Saimara, the queen of his inner heart. His one and only her. Bairoop knew very well, she wasn't buried where the hieroglyphs said she was, back in the old country.

***

Though Bairoop didn't really care for the smell of these new mortals, he had to force himself to be close to these sweating hordes of humanity in this museum. As Bairoop made his way through the crowds of this most visited museum in Londonium, the statues of friends and foes whispered to him, as always. Almost all the Egyptians murmured in the Old Tongue, begging their emperor for a drop of the precious Nile water. They were so thirsty. It was painful to him, and he tried to pretend he wasn't able to hear them. The Phrygians, the Hittites, and the Thracians all wanted him to free them from their statues, so that they could challenge him to a one-to-one battle. But he knew that wasn't the real reason they wanted to be free. They'd run away as soon as he'd set their spirits free.

***

Ignoring all these annoying whisperings, hands behind his back, Bairoop strolled along. He took the long route to Saimara's bust. Bairoop blamed himself for her demise. Why did he have to lead some stupid war campaign himself, that had seemed so important at that time, leaving Saimara to fend for herself? If only he hadn't been away from her, she'd still be by his side for all these millennia. He was sure her body had been looted by bold conquerors, mainly for her jewels smuggled away to these cursed inhospitable lands

She could have defended herself, but for the scheming, greedy priests; too open to bribery. Not to mention bodyguards, her personal slaves. All colluding through fear, or avidity. All of them reduced to nothingness before his rage upon his return.

Even as he'd mourned her for the next few centuries, he knew this knife-like longing that was stuck like an orichalcum dagger in his heart would never really go away. No one on this cursed planet would ever be able to understand their love for each other. When their souls had been united, they had floated amongst the stars. Experienced things these mortals couldn't even conceive of in their mundane existence, and limited dreams.

Some took him for a tramp, a wanderer, or a beggar. It didn't matter. No one knew who he'd been just after the first century had passed, after her *ka* and *ba* had floated away from her perfect body. The long line of priests sworn to serve him tried their best to look after him, but he could never stay confined in one place. He kept moving on. But he knew that his personal guards were never too far behind.

Soon after his darling Saimara had been murdered, had he been wrong not to defend his people, his cities, palaces, forts, way of life?

But in the listless grey world that had dragged on after her passing, nothing had any value left for him. He'd wanted to float away too in order to join her in the Afterworld, but the priests had advised strongly against. He had to stay here, and follow the will of the gods. Fulfil his destiny. Who knew what was written in the stars for him?

***

So he'd gotten himself interred in a sarcophagus for a few centuries, hoping that there'd be a malfunction and that either he'd expire inside it, or that tomb robbers would cause his death. But he was disappointed to re-emerge about two millennia later. The entire world had changed around him, but his core team of priests and guards, those who knew of his otherworldly blood had passed on the instructions assiduously from father to son, to open the sarcophagus at the right time in the correct way.

He'd been lost and uncaring for a few decades, and still had no great desire to live. But his priests always told him, he had to keep on wandering the surface of this hellish globe until fate decided otherwise.

Then, the son of his Chief Guard had timidly shown him a book of Egyptian antiquities in a distant land somewhere, hoping to distract the Lost Emperor. And he'd almost stopped breathing! Her photo had caught his eye. There was nothing left to live for, except for this warm, rose-colored bust that had been labelled wrong. He'd begun preparations at once to travel to this inhospitably inhospitable land.

***

At long last, here he was once more, like every year after discovering the photo of her bust quite by accident. 'Hete-tipi' wasn't her real name. It didn't matter that they couldn't really read the pre-dynastic hieroglyphs correctly. He guarded his precious secret of knowing her real name, her slanting half smiles, how her gurgles mingled with the stream's murmurs on their private tours of the Bird Islands on their sacred Nile. The colour of her eyes painted orange by eternal sunsets. He'd have joined her long ago in the Great Hereafter if he hadn't been forbidden to do so by the augury. by the seeresses, by the sooth-sayers, by the wretched priests, but most of all, by her.

In those precious dreams when she came to brush his existence with the light touch of her whited out flowing robes. Gave him the courage to drag himself through yet another miserable century somehow.

***

"Psst! Shahenshah! Watch out! To your left! Go to your right now!" The friendly Persian youth whispered loudly from across the hall. Only Bairoop could hear these

91

unspoken whispers in his head. Bairoop resisted looking to his left, and smartly turned right. He looked at his watch, as if he were late, before picking up his pace. Bairoop risked a look at his followers from between the forest of busts and statues. He could have picked out this trio in any crowd. Strong, muscular men. Bent on business. Part of the Secret Paranormal Police Force. Somehow, they'd gotten word he'd be there, visiting his precious lady that day.

His sixth sense kicked in. They were fanning out behind him now. He could feel their heavy energy behind him.

"Quick! Come here, Imperator!" the old Etruscan statue whispered. "Hide behind me, and wait till they pass!" Somehow, all the statues could feel who he was. Since he wasn't arrogant or proud like their own rulers, they respected him the more for that.

Bairoop quickly ducked behind the Etruscan's high sarcophagus. Two old ladies gazed at him curiously. Bairoop quickly took off his frayed grey jacket, turned it inside out, and wore it again so that the dark blue checked side was visible now. He put on a dark blue hat. Would that throw off his stalkers? No. They weren't mere humans these predators. They had the noses of a Dobermann. They could smell the golden ichor mixed in his human blood from a mile away.

As Bairoop passed into the next hall, the hostile

Phrygians tried to tell his location to the predators, but luckily they couldn't hear them. A Roman general, who detested Egyptians was even shouting to the policemen, but to no avail. The head of an unknown plebeian nearly winked at Bairoop. But Bairoop had no time to stop and wonder at this unusual statue. A little girl with intense blue eyes was looking from the Roman General, to Bairoop, to the pleb. Could she hear their whispering? A mere mortal child? But there was no time to investigate this mortal's capabilities.

Bairoop heard a crash behind him. And heard the pleb laughing, with the Roman general shouting at him. Apparently, the statue had put out his foot at the last minute, tripping up one of the bull-dog faced men following Bairoop. The other two had been too astonished to come after Bairoop. The blue-eyed child started giggling loudly. Had she seen the pleb do his trick?

Almost sprinting, Bairoop had reached the next gallery. But he was in a panic now. He didn't want to be caught by these goons. Not because he was afraid for himself, but because there'd be no one to visit his beloved Saimara's bust on their special day. In fact, it was well-known amongst all the statues that she was the only one who got a special flesh and ichor visitor every year. But somehow, she never spoke to him. Remained enigmatically silent. Perhaps she wanted to discourage him from risking his royal neck by visiting her, but he'd been ignoring her silent treatment for years now. In the beginning, he'd left small bouquets of magenta petunias or blue irises, but it had become too risky to do so. It was like asking the Paranormal Police to be on the lookout for him next year on the same date. All they wanted from him was the location of his treasure. And he was never going to give away the real site of Saimara's tomb.

***

"Go to the middle of the Hall, and turn right. There are swing doors leading to another gallery. They're protected by Trojan guards, but they'll yield to your touch. Just give them the code words of *Hectorius respirata, Hectorius vivada!*" the head of an unknown Anatolian woman whispered to Bairoop.

Luckily, the metallic Trojan guards who'd been standing immobile with their crossed spears blocking the hidden doors to the next gallery withdrew their spears on hearing the code words. The doors yielded at Bairoop's touch. But as soon as Bairoop entered the next gallery, his heart sank. It wasn't as thickly populated as the others. Was this a trick so that his pursuers would spot him more quickly? He'd changed his clothes, in a manner of speaking, but perhaps his tall height, and full, royal head gave him away. Also, his pursuers had a keen sense of smell, and there was nothing much he could do to disguise the scent of his immortal blood. Luckily, the doors of this cold gallery shut with a comforting click.

"Scribe Papayree at your service. Sorry am I that I can't bow before your Majesty," a full-sized Egyptian scribe began apologizing in the Ancient Tongue. Made of clay, he was sitting cross-legged, wearing thin cotton clothes. His desk and writing implements were set out before him.

"There's no time to stand on ceremony. Quick! Tell me, is there a safe way to exit this museum?" Bairoop whispered back.

"Sorry am I that I don't know. But should the High Effendi ask the Seeress Laclaire of Thaluna in the next gallery, she may help the High Effendi." Scribe Papayree would have scraped his hands together, if he could have. Bairoop could feel Papayree's regret that he couldn't help him more. Bairoop was almost running now. There were no tourists in here. Also, it was dusty, as if this gallery wasn't cleaned much. Perhaps the public wasn't allowed in these galleries. He hoped the goons would assume he'd gone onto the next public gallery, and not barge in here.

"We wish so much that we could help Your Majesty too!" a couple of Nubian guards made of basalt, holding spears piped up from behind Papayree. They were dressed in short, thigh-length leather tunics, with matching mid-calf leather pants, and sandals.

***

As soon as he entered the adjoining gallery, the scent of incense struck his nostrils. Though her head was calm, and serene, it attracted his attention at once. Made of white alabaster, peace flowed around her head.

"Panic not, our friend, our Great Protector!" she whispered. And Bairoop knew that only he could hear her, and not any of the other statues in these galleries. He hid behind a tall statue of a warrior, close to her head.

"They won't find you here quite that easily. Their sense of smell won't serve them in here." she whispered.

"Who are you?" Bairoop whispered back.

"Don't you know that already from your faithful Scribe Papayree?" the Seeress of Thaluna asked.

"How can you help me? I need to get out of this infernal museum." Bairoop wished she'd hurry.

"Worry not, our Great Protector. All in good time," she whispered in measured tones.

"Even if those goons don't find me in here, they're likely to catch me with their infernal seeing machines as soon as I try to exit this cold, lifeless museum," Bairoop wanted to be sure she understood his plight clearly.

"Your Goodness, the mortals haven't progressed so much that they can outwit both of us. The Seeress of Thaluna will be glad to be of use, if Your Graceful Highness could help her too."

"And how exactly am I supposed to do that?"

"If Your Serenity would be so kind as to wrap my head in your pristine white muslin scarf, and swear on the sacred blue lotuses of the Nile never to abandon me, then I can indeed help us both to exit this accursed place safely." the Seeress said smoothly.

"Never to abandon you? What does that mean? That I'd be saddled with you forever?" Bairoop whispered hoarsely. He was used to being on his own, to travelling lightly. Not to be saddled with a stolen museum piece.

"Oh, if Your Serene Highness could fulfil seven of my wishes, then you may deposit me at a certain destination. And you'd be free after that, Seeress Laclaire promises you that much." she said smoothly.

"Seven wishes? Isn't that a lot? I mean, couldn't you just help me get out of here, without adding all these conditions? Aren't seeresses meant to help people, anyway?" Bairoop tried to keep the irritation out of his voice.

"I'm afraid Your Serenity, I wouldn't have asked you for

these favours, if I could have avoided it. But now we have to help each other, don't we?"

A loud thwack sounded from faraway. Were the goons trying to force their way in? Bairoop the Trojan guards wouldn't let them enter the adjoining gallery.

"All right, all right! You've given me no choice, I suppose." Bairoop picked up the head and wrapped it in his scarf. A few more thwacking sounds came from behind the closed doors of the gallery. Were the goons trying to force their way in?

"But first you must take the Scribe Papayree with you. If you touch his heart and recite the words he tells you to, your royal words and breath will bring him to life." The voice from the Seeress's head was clear enough.

Keeping the wrapped head of the Seeress Laclaire back on its pedestal, Bairoop didn't waste time arguing with her. As soon as he'd finished reciting the ancient poem, Papayaree shuddered into life. He began sneezing and coughing uncontrollably.

"Please Sire! Our King! Our Merciful Emperor! Please give life to us too! We beg of you! We'll serve you well! We swear on the lives of our grandchildren!" the Nubian guards began pleading with him in their charming, musical voices.

"They'll be useful for us, Your Serenity!" Seeress

Laclaire's voice floated in effortlessly from her head. Bairoop thought they could be serviceable, too. Specially as his personal guards had been taken by the Paranormal Police Force. He brought the Nubians to life with the help of Papayaree's spell.

"And could Your Graciousness pick up that statue of that Indian monkey too, if it pleases you?" the Seeress requested. Suwi, the Nubian guard, picked up the monkey called Kuchi, dressed in faded orange Indian clothes. Rashad, the other guard, helped a shaky Papayree along, who insisted on folding up his desk and taking all his implements as well. So, Rashad snatched a big satchel from a nearby cowboy statue, who shouted at this 'theft,' and stuffing the desk and the implements in it, Rashad carried it on his own back.

***

"Where to now?" Bairoop was fast losing patience with all the requests of the Seeress. Kuchi the monkey was chattering away brightly, now that he'd been given the breath of life as well.

"If Your Graciousness would place your royal hand over the lock of that door, and if Scribe Papayree could tell you the words to bend metal to your iron will, then it will open, Your Serenity!" Seeress Laclaire enunciated each word carefully. The sounds of thwacking became more frequent, more urgent from behind the doors.

"Worry not, Your Majesty. The Trojan Guards are loyal to us, and no one can beat them in a fair fight." Seeress Laclaire soothed them all with her calm tone.

A solid-looking metal door. But Bairoop had no choice but to try it. Papayree was so nervous, he tripped up his spell three times before the lock clicked open. Yawning before them was a dark set of stairs going down.

"Where's the light switch?" Bairoop had become so used to modern life that he expected electricity to be everywhere. But no switches were to be seen anywhere, and he didn't have a torch.

"If it so pleases Your Serenity, could you remove the scarf from my face?" the Seeress didn't seem to be in a hurry to get away from there. As Bairoop did so, she began reciting a spell. Gradually, her eyes light up with a blue light. Bairoop lifted her head. Her eyes lit up the passageway, though quite faintly.

Suwi, the Nubian guard with the long curly hair bravely led the way into the semi-darkness, step by step, followed by Bairoop, the Scribe, with Rashad carrying the monkey on his shoulder brought up the rear, holding up the Seeress's head for those in front to see by her light. From time to time, Rashad had to stop Kuchi from pulling at his long gold earrings, which glinted even in the eerie blue light.

***

As Rashad closed the door behind them, Bairoop couldn't help giving a sigh of relief. All they had to do now was to find their way out of the labyrinth underneath the museum. Somehow, he had a feeling the mysterious Seeress Laclaire would be able to help him to find his way to the cold, fresh air outside, and to freedom for all of them.

CLEARING A PATH

D.L. SMITH-LEE

The guards' heads darted from left to right, trying to catch sight of the lightning fast shadow as it rushed past. The preceding nights brought a few intruders, but this one was different. None ever made it past the impervious force shields that surrounded the Embassy, one of many underground resistance quarters. The second anyone or anything crossed the shields without permission, they instantly faltered beneath its weight like an ant feebly at the bottom of a boot. The shields were invisible to the untrained eye, so whoever had crossed was no ordinary man. The four guards stood back to back, quivering. They were among the few guards who survived tonight's invasion. The Embassy's secrets could not fall into the wrong hands. Whoever the intruder was, they'd already seen too much.

They'd chased the shadow into a storage room, suspecting that it led them there. Though they tried to warn the General assigned to command their battalion, she dismissed their claims and ordered them after it. Wisplights floated freely throughout the room like fireflies, casting their pale bluish gleam off the walls. The shadow zoomed by once more, casting itself on the dim, white walls.

"It went over there," said Cassius, pointing a finger to a dark corner.

"Go get it," ordered Donn, the highest in rank of the four. Cassius immediately obeyed, knowing there would be consequences had he not. Carefully tip toeing through the darkness, he drew his blade. The unearthly pinkish glow of the blade emitted into the places the dim wisplights missed. After slowly weaving through small piles of crates, Cassius reached the corner, seeing nothing but the filthy walls stained with marks from who knows what. A sigh of relief escaped his mouth as he sheathed his sword. He turned to yell back to the other guards, but a callous, heavy hand slapped over his lips and another shoved him against the wall.

"Filthy mortal," the assailant hissed at the guard. Cassius' hand reached for his blade, but something strange about the assailant's eyes made him stop. The golden glow they emitted was dizzying. Cassius watched the rigid rings of gold revolve in the man's eyes, dancing gracefully around the pitch-black pupil that seemed the grow and stretch with the sporadic twitching of a convulsing corpse. Cassius couldn't stop looking into the man's eyes. He knew he should've called for the captain to slaughter this monster wrapped in flesh, but its eyes were so...golden. And the black of them called out to Cassius with a yearning Cassius didn't understand. It was as if everything around them had stopped.

"Is it back there?" another guard called, but it was as if he'd yelled it from across a field. All Cassius heard was the whisper of the assailant. Cassius knew what this assailant was; one of the demons sent to expose their Embassy.

"Squirm for me," the demon whispered. Cassius began to feel his mind sink toward the man's eyes. The golden glow faded as black inky fluid oozed down his cheeks. A drop of the liquid landed on Cassius' hand and it spread over his skin. He could feel it creeping across his hand moving up his arm. The demon removed his weight from Cassius and watched as the blackness overtook his arm, moving to the rest of his body. Cassius screamed, falling to the ground scratching away at the blackness, but it wouldn't go away. He looked up, but the demon was no longer there. The other guards ran to his rescue, weaving through the crates, locating him in the corner where they thought the shadow had gone. Cassius was frantically scratching his arm, scraping off the skin.

"What the hell are you doing?" asked Donn.

"It's everywhere!" Cassius screamed, squirming wildly. "It's everywhere!" He could still see it, the blackness covered most of his biceps now and would not stop.

"What are you talking about? Stop damn it, you're bleeding!"

The others couldn't see the blackness. They'd forgotten about the shadow, rushing toward Cassius to restrict his arms. Cassius saw the demon materialize behind the other guards, looking down at the guards as they tried to calm their panicking comrade. The demon's eyes turned black once more, the black teardrops fell to the ground and slithered across the floor like mutant ivy over the side of a house. The guards noticed the inky liquid spreading and turned to find the demon.

"You," said the captain, drawing his blade. "You son of a bitch! What have you done to him?!"

The demon remained silent. The captain felt something

slippery at his feet. He looked down and saw an enormous snake slithering leisurely up his leg. He halted, fearing he may upset it.

"I fear he is the least of your worries, captain," the demon said. Donn saw the ground now littered with more slippery scaled reptiles, weaving cold tangled nests at his men's feet. The snakes wrapped around the men like binding chains, hissing as the guards struggled to free themselves. Donn fell to his knees, his heart throbbing in his chest. The demon stood over Donn, a devilish grin spread across his face. Before he could say anything, the demon took hold of both sides of Donn's face and crushed their lips together. The captain's eyes grew wide with astonishment. He could feel a sensation at the back of his throat he'd thought to be vomit, tickling itself free. It curled and twitched in his esophagus and Donn could only think to puke at the taste of the foul tang. The demon removed his lips from Donn's and allowed him to belch out the serpent he'd planted in his throat. Donn would have screamed, but the serpent encased his head with its body as it continued to slither from his mouth.

While the guards lay incapacitated, the demon snatched the captain's sword.

"Pure, ornate blades, wisplights to illuminate the darkness, and *almost* impenetrable force fields to protect you," he said. "Now what traitorous little *demon* could've given you all this?"

The guards squirmed helplessly on the ground as the snakes bound their bodies and covered their mouths. The demon smiled sadistically and planted the blade into each guard's chest, taking pleasure as they writhed in anguish. He didn't need their answer. He knew the name of the traitor who'd aided their mortal enemies and turned against his own kind. Demons is what these mortals had come to call them. Other names followed; fiends, Spawns of Satan, Hellspawn. The latter he found most amusing because he was closer to the sons of God than anywhere near the Christian Hell. He was, in fact a descendant of the sons of God, one of the Nephilim. And he'd chosen his own name after The Descent: Usiel.

After Usiel wiped the blood from the shining blade, he pocketed it for later. He knew there would be more of these foolhardy mortal guards. Perhaps he would even get the pleasure of slaying the leader appointed to their battalion, or even the traitor.

Usiel condensed himself into his shadow form once more, creeping across the walls. He slid under the door and out to the dark corridor. There he materialized into his human form and surveyed the hall silently. The corridor split into two directions.

Where the hell are you, Zazriel? he thought to himself.

As he stood deliberating in the silent shadows, a blinding shot of light struck him, knocking him backwards into a wall. He sat up, adjusting his eyes to the darkness to see from where the blast came. A slender figure emerged from the shadows, walking slowly in his direction. The sheen of his silvery mane of hair gathered the wisplights around him, illuminating his pallid face. Usiel immediately identified him.

"Pathiel," he said as the angel came to a halt.

"So you know me," said Pathiel. "It doesn't matter either way."

Usiel tried to transform himself back to shadow form, but he couldn't. His body felt too heavy to lift.

"What have you done to me?"

"You are the one called Usiel, correct?" Pathiel asked, ignoring Usiel's question and closing the distance between them. "But that isn't your real name, now is it? I think I will really enjoy killing you slowly."

A grin formed across the angel's face as multiple mortal guards wielding the same glowing blades surrounded him, halting for orders.

"Take him to the cells," Pathiel ordered.

***

Usiel grew irritable as he laid in his cell. He couldn't believe he'd been overpowered by the traitor that aided their enemies. There were hundreds of mortals lurking about these caverns and they were receiving help and protection from Pathiel.

At the bars of his cell stood a young man—a boy, really—who couldn't be much older than twenty years of age. The blade he wore at his side told Usiel that he was another guard. Usiel was immediately reminded of the facilities where mortals once gathered to view captured animals in cages. Menageries, they called them. Was that what this place was?

He removed his forearm from his eyes and glared at the mortal man.

"How long do you plan to stand there, mortal?" he asked. The man flinched. His lips trembled as though the words were dancing in his mouth, but he couldn't spit them out. The young man probably hadn't expected him to speak.

"Well?" Usiel demanded again.

The young man frowned and swallowed nervously, crossing his arms.

"Do you have a problem with it?" he shot back. A wicked chuckle escaped Usiel's throat. He was genuinely tickled by the audacity of this tiny mortal man.

"Do not try to feign bravery, human. It's more pathetic than being a coward," he said before resting his forearm over his eyes again.

Where the hell is Zazriel? he asked himself.

"Trying to make conversation with it is futile," said an older male voice. A fire boiled in Usiel's stomach at the word "it". He recognized this as the voice of Pathiel. This type of slight was typical of those who were "fully" angel before The Descent. The Fallen Ones had long since embraced their Nephilim descendants, but there were pockets of them—like Pathiel—who still bore a grudge against Nephilim like Usiel, since they were not fully angel and not fully human. Angels like Pathiel hadn't cared that even humans rejected the Nephilim as monstrosities, perversions of nature. Usiel got to his feet and walked to the bars of his cell.

"Your traitorous ways are unbounded, I see," said Usiel.

Pathiel frowned at him.

"The only reason you are not dead is that I need information. The Descent was disgraceful. Angels were never meant to live on Earth, let alone rule humanity," Pathiel said.

Usiel knew what information he had been referencing: Pathiel needed a way into the City. Like his Fallen brethren,

Pathiel's wings had been severed from his back long ago. But when he turned against the Fallen in favor of humanity he had been cut from their collective mind—the link that bonded the Fallen Ones to each other. He had no way back into the City, its impervious shields and massive walls barring his path. The mortals he attempted to lead wouldn't dare go near it without him.

"And what makes you think for a moment that I will give you any information?"

"I didn't request your cooperation."

Before Usiel could react, Pathiel hit him again with the same blast, crippling him against the cell wall.

***

The mortal guards threw Usiel into the chair with more force than necessary. He supposed it satisfied the mortals too, for once, overpower the beings considered more powerful than they were. The chains that bound Usiel to his seat wouldn't have been able to hold him had Pathiel not had the ability to negate his powers as he did.

"Well, is this your master plan?" he asked Pathiel, chuckling. Pathiel bent down before him at eye level.

"You needn't worry," Pathiel said before walking behind him. Usiel suddenly saw flashbacks of his home. The multicolored stone towers of the City glowed before his eyes. The metropolis had once been ruled by mortals before coming under the angels' rule. The cowardice ruler of this mortal country had abandoned this metropolis.

Who in the right mind would stand against us? Usiel thought.

Ahead of him, Usiel could see the fifty-foot-high statue of the man presenting a sword in his palms, the hilt in one hand and the blade in the other with his wings fully expanded. Semyaza. Beneath the gloom of the clouded skies, the statue's eyes were cast downward through the assault of colors, watching his children.

At Usiel's side was his mortal slave. He'd bought this mortal man at an auction just outside of the Hives, a place where mortals once gathered en masse. On the opposite side of Usiel stood...

The memory became hazy before Usiel's eyes. Blackness covered his vision.

"You can try to block me out all you want," Pathiel's voice called through the darkness. Usiel grunted furiously as he tried to pry the angel from his thoughts.

Zazriel, he thought.

Another memory came, a memory of dark tunnels. The passageways led up into dark hallways littered with dim wisplights. One passage led to a room filled with crates where four corpses had laid for hours. No one had acknowledged the men's bodies on their hunt for the intruder. The cavernous hallways led to the massive foyer where the dungeons lay just beyond. Two stairwells diverged and reconnected to a singular passageway leading to a guarded room at its end.

Pathiel recognized the Embassy and realized that this was a recent memory.

"You conjure a memory of this Embassy to block me out?" said Pathiel, scoffing. Usiel smiled at the traitor's words. Triumph flushed through him at the revelation that Pathiel had gotten.

"It's not a memory. I've only cleared a path for them."

"What?"

Before Pathiel could inquire anything further, Usiel could hear the familiar sound of splatter behind him as Pathiel's body hit the ground. Usiel could hear the commotion from below, the screams of the mortals as the denizens of his home had arrived.

He heard the loud footsteps of the Nephilim that had disposed of his captor walk around to stand before him. The beautiful olive-toned male Nephilim of gleaming golden eyes, like Usiel's, smiled down at him.

"Took you long enough," Zazriel said to Usiel.

"Could say the same about you," Usiel said. Zazriel leaned down to kiss his lover as if for the first time, the reek of the accursed traitor's blood assailing Usiel's nostrils. As their lips met, they could feel one another's memories. Usiel could feel the torturous wounds in Zazriel's skin that had been carved into him as punishment for withholding information, but they hesitated to kill him. This was likely to Pathiel's sadistic pleasure. Zazriel pulled away from their kiss. Usiel looked up to Zazriel, observing the dried bloody wounds with his own eyes. He felt himself ready to cry, wanting to caress his lover's scars and nurse him back to health. But Zazriel was strong, Usiel knew it.

"If you ever kiss another mortal, I'll rip out your tongue," said Zazriel.

Usiel grinned as Zazriel freed him.

***

The caves, baptized in the blood of the mortals who dared stand against the Nephilim, had fallen silent. The howls of the wind reverberated from the empty walls as their cries for help were drowned in their earthly prison.

Usiel grinned in the silent darkness with his lover beside him. The mortals' cries were musical, melodious to their ears. The two condensed themselves into the shadows, making their way above to cross the barren wasteland that would lead them back home to the City.

HEAVENFIRE

SPENCER HELSEL

Little could be heard over the downpour blanketing the city. If someone was near the alley, they would hear the footfalls through the puddles, the screams, and the growls of something inhuman.

There were five; two children, fleeing down a dead-end between two buildings, and the three that followed them. The three were the hardest to see. The rain masked them in gloom, and yet, something else kept them hidden. The overhead streetlights couldn't pierce the shadows over their faces. There was nothing definitive about them; like walking silhouettes, featureless, save for the smell of sulfur.

But their movements were unmistakable. They were predators, stalking their prey, which cowered before them.

The two little ones trembled. As the three got closer, one called out, "Leave us alone!"

The three growled.

The taller of the two youngsters, a boy of only eleven or twelve, stepped in front of the other, a girl. He held out his hand, which gave the three stalkers pause.

"Stay away!" he warned, terror in his voice.

It was as if the three dark figures expected the boy to do something, but when nothing happened, they continued to approach.

"I said stay away!"

But the attackers charged. Confident in their kill, they howled. Milky, white eyes glared from the darkness of their faces, along with a glint of razor-sharp teeth. They leapt toward their prey in a distance that should've been impossible.

But they couldn't grab the two children. Before they could, something dropped between them and let out a burst of blue-white light. The blast exploded rainwater and hurtled the three into a skid across the alley.

The blast blinded the two children. The boy heard a sound like a hiss of steam and then light poured into the darkness. The figure who saved them stormed through the rain, with something like fire in their hand. The flames were a warm blue that hissed as they touched the rain. They were dressed in a jacket with the hood up, swinging the flames like a sword at the three dark figures and fighting them off.

Another person dropped next to the children. Then a third. The second ran to join the fight, but the third turned to them.

Her eyes were the greenest the boy and girl had ever seen. Sodden hair clung to her face, but despite everything, she smiled warmly at them.

"Are you alright?" she asked tenderly.

The boy was still shaking. So was the girl.

"Hey, it's okay," she told them, smoothing a hand down both their arms reassuringly. "We won't let them hurt you."

"Everlee!" someone warned.

The blonde savior turned. One dark figure had made it to the end of the alley. It snarled, its white eyes wide with rage.

The blonde extended her hand and blue-white fire unfurled into her palm. Extending it, she hurtled a flaming bolt through the darkness. The thing dodged, dropped to hands and feet, and scurried forward. The girl ran at it. The two collided and tumbled to the ground.

Blue flames pierced the night. Someone screamed. But there were also the unholy howls of the creatures in darkness and the stench of ignited sulfur. Red-orange flames leapt out and there was a second, bloody cry of pain, followed by more shouts.

The blonde girl wrestled the creature, grabbing for its back. It stood, trying to shake her off. Then, as if igniting the night, blue flames swirled around her body. Her green eyes lit aflame. She shoved the creature down to its knees, bowed its head, and then twisted upward across its neck. With a sickening snap! the neck

118

broke, and the creature fell.

Another howl and, through the darkness, one of the black figures bisected in half. Blue flame cut through, revealing another hooded figure. The alleyway went silent.

The blonde girl returned to the two children. "Are you two okay? Did any of them hurt you?"

The boy shook his head. The girl cried.

"It's okay, honey. They're gone. I promise."

"Everlee!" a male voice called out.

"What is it?"

"It's Grace! She's hurt!"

The blonde girl left and raced back down the alleyway. The stench of burnt sulfur choked the air. She coughed, covering her mouth, but then she let out a strangled wail. She dropped onto the asphalt beside the prone form of the third hooded savior. She picked her up into her arms, casting back the hood.

"Grace? Grace, can you hear me?" The one called Everlee asked.

The children stood slowly, approaching. As they passed one of the dark figures, they saw that it was dissolving in the rain, melting into mist and shadow.

Their gaze fell on the three. Grace was a brunette with pale eyes. Bright, red blood streamed from a wound in her side into a storm-drain and ran in torrents across her face from a gaping hole in her neck. Part of her jawline on the other side was burn-scarred. Her mouth moved, but no words came.

"Shh, shh, don't try to talk," Everlee told her. She looked to her companion. "Mason, we need to get her back to the Sanctuary."

Mason, a boy of no more than twenty, with golden-brown eyes and dark hair said nothing.

"We can help her," Everlee said with a voice that cracked with desperation. "There has to be a way… she's lost so much blood, but maybe we can… we can…" It was like the knowledge of what was about to happen was too painful to voice. Even as Everlee looked down at Grace, she didn't want to say it; as if it would cause it to happen.

But it happened anyway. The life that lit behind Grace's eyes faded. Her breathing slowed. And, in her last moments, she squeezed Everlee's hand in her own, until there was no strength left and it slipped to the ground.

Then Grace was dead, and the only sound was the rain and Everlee's sobs.

***

"My name is Everlee. This is Mason," she said.

They took the children to a nearby diner. It was quiet there, save for the sounds of clattering dishes and hushed conversation of the few diner patrons. The mood was solemn, but neither Mason nor Everlee talked about what they felt. Instead, they spoke to the two children, who were visibly shaken by the encounter. "What are your names?"

The boy spoke. "I'm Dillion. This is Ivy."

"I know you both have a lot of questions, but we don't have long," she told them.

"Long before what?"

"Before the wraiths find you again."

"Wraiths?"

"The things in the alley."

Dillion held Ivy's hand, as Everlee had when taking them out of the alley. Comfortingly. Protectively.

Everlee noticed. "You were very brave back there, Dillion."

"They weren't human, were they?" He made it a question, but only to confirm what he already knew.

"No," Mason answered. "They were demons."

"Demons? You mean, as in Hell?"

"Yes."

The girl sobbed quietly.

"What did they want?" Dillion asked.

"You," Mason answered. "Or, one of you, at least."

"Mason," Everlee hissed angrily. "We don't tell them before they get to the Sanctuary."

He snorted in derision.

"We have people who can tell you everything," Everlee explained to the kids. "There's a safe place we can take you: The Sanctuary. We just need to get you to—."

"I want to know now," Ivy spoke for the first time. She met Everlee's gaze. She was terrified. "Please."

Everlee glanced at Mason, who muttered, "I say tell them. I've never been a fan of hiding it from the new ones."

"The Sanctuary leaders know how best to explain."

"Really? You think there's a better way of explaining Purgatory?"

"Purgatory?" Dillion caught the word.

The two protectors became silent.

Mason said softly, "Grace gave her life to save them. They should know.."

Everlee sighed, "Fine." She leaned across the table. "Have either of you noticed something wrong with this city? Like, how it's always gloomy, or how there's no direct sunlight, even during the day? Or, how it's uncomfortably cold all the time?"

Neither answered, but a light of recognition sparked.

"That's because this city, this place, it's not really… real."

"Not real?"

"This isn't life," Mason said, not one to beat around the bush. "I'm sorry to tell you, but you're dead."

"Dead?" Dillion asked.

"Yeah. Sorry about your bad luck, kid."

Ivy sniffed back tears.

"You could've been gentler," Everlee told him, "but, Mason's right. You, us, anyone in this city; we're all dead."

"But I remember——." Ivy started to say.

"Moving here?" Mason cut her off. "Where you're from? Who your parents are? You may have a few vague memories, but nothing really concrete, right?"

Their silence was confirmation.

"That's because death is traumatic. Everyone mostly forgets their life when they die. Don't worry, though. It wouldn't matter. Most of us are orphans."

"Us?"

"Nephilim."

Neither of the two recognized the term.

Everlee explained, "Nephilim are the sons and daughters of a human and an angel."

"I'm an angel?" Ivy squeaked.

"No, just the mutt from one," Mason grumbled.

"Mason!" Everlee smacked his arm. "No, honey, you're not an angel. Neither are we." She leaned in closer. "Nephilim are the offspring of a human woman and a Fallen angel in mortal form."

Mason added, "Like mules are the offspring of a donkey and a horse. We're half-breeds."

"Nice analogy," Everlee grumbled.

"Pretty accurate, given we can't have children."

"I don't understand," Dillion said. "Nephilim, Purgatory; how does this make sense? You said we're dead. If we're part-angel, shouldn't we go to Heaven?"

"And there's the cosmic joke," Mason muttered.

Everlee shot him a warning look, but softened when she spoke to the kids. "There's no easy way to say this, but no, you wouldn't. Purgatory is an in-between world; one between life and the afterlife. It's… limbo. Everyone here," she nodded at the other patrons, "are souls unclaimed by Heaven or Hell. They're dead, but they don't know it, like you. Because this is undecided territory, demons can enter. The ones you saw, the wraiths, prey on souls, and they especially like Nephilim. We're…" she didn't know how to describe it.

"Tastier," Mason finished for her. "Another wonderful side effect of being part-angelic."

"But our parents were Fallen angels," Everlee went on. "They left Heaven, so they can't go back. And because we are their offspring, neither can we."

"But that's not fair!" Ivy whimpered.

"Preaching to the choir, kid," Mason grunted, finishing his coffee. "Since we're angelic, though, Hell can't claim us, either. So, when we die, we end up here. Purgatory: Heaven and Hell's landfill."

"You're not making this better," Everlee told him.

"Am I supposed to? We didn't — hell, they didn't! — do anything wrong in life, and yet they get stuck in this place as prey for monsters."

"Mason, they're kids! Stop being so cruel!"

"This place is cruel, Everlee. I'm just being honest."

The two broke into an argument, for a moment forgetting about the kids.

Dillion, however, turned his attention to Ivy. She was still crying, and he squeezed her hand for comfort. "It'll be okay," he told her.

"We died," she sniffled. "How is that okay?"

"It's not," he admitted, but gave her his best smile, "but we're together. We found each other. Hey, look at me," he said, touching her chin, "I don't know you and you don't know me, but I do know we'll be okay. I won't let anything happen to you."

Ivy smiled, sniffing back tears. "Okay."

Everlee finally held up a hand, cutting Mason off. "Enough!" She noticed the two across the table and visibly grimaced in embarrassment. "I'm sorry. It's just, Mason and I have been here a long time; no telling how long, actually. We've seen a lot of friends die, like Grace."

"They died fighting the monsters?" Ivy asked.

Everlee nodded.

"If we die, what happens to us?"

"We don't know. No one does."

"But, if demons are here," Dillion said, "then why don't the angels—?"

"Kid," Mason cut him off, "you're asking the same question a hundred other Nephilim have asked. We don't got an answer. Sorry."

Ivy asked softly, "If you're part angel, then is that how you did the thing with the fire?"

Everlee smiled. "We call it heavenfire," she explained. "It's one of the few things we can do against wraiths. Demons, you see, use hellfire. It burns like brimstone—like sulfur, I mean. But we aren't demons. We summon," she held up her hand, "heavenfire."

Blue-white flames flicked between her fingers into a ball in her palm. The glow was warm and despite it being fire, it wasn't terrifying. It was almost comforting, like a campfire on a cold night.

She extinguished the flames. "We'll teach you," she said. "I promise."

"Well, we'll teach one of you," Mason added.

Dillion frowned. "One of us?"

"Only one of you is a Nephilim."

"I don't understand."

Everlee licked her lips nervously. "We Nephilim can sense each other, to an extent. We can tell when one of us enters Purgatory, and can find them. But, sometimes, it's difficult when we're around shades."

"Shades?"

"Non-Nephilim in Purgatory. Lost souls. We sensed you. That's why we came. That's why Grace was so adamant to find you. There hasn't been a new Nephilim in Purgatory in a long time. We rushed to find you, but," she glanced at Mason, "we're not sure which of you is actually the Nephilim and which of you is just a shade."

Dillion squeezed Ivy's hand tighter. "Is there a way to tell?"

She nodded. "The wraiths came after you because one of you used a Nephilim power, like heavenfire. Wraiths are attracted to it, like moths to a flame." She glanced between them. "Did either of you do something you didn't mean to?"

Dillion shook his head. Ivy was silent.

"Well, we can figure it out with a simple test with my heavenfire. We can see which of you responds to it, and that'll be the one who is really a Nephilim. But, we need to hurry, before the wraiths—."

She paused. Both she and Mason cocked their heads to the side. Then, turning, they stared back out one of the windows into the black, drizzling night.

For a moment, neither spoke, but then stood up in unison.

"They're here," Everlee said.

"What is?"

"Wraiths."

"How do you know?" Dillion asked.

Ivy mewled in terror.

"We can sense them. Get behind us," Mason told them, pouring a ball of flame into his hand. "Everlee is going to stick close to you. We're going to get out of here. Back to the Sanctuary."

Everlee's flames flowed outward into the unmistakable form of a long, curved sword. She held it out to the side, between the window and the children.

The other people in the diner fled. It went quiet. In the hush, the only sound was the remaining meat sizzling on the griddle in the back and hum of air conditioning.

The quiet was unnerving.

Dillion stood with Ivy, still holding hands. He tried to see what

Everlee and Mason saw through the windows, but there was nothing. Their eyes were fixed on one window; one direction.

But then, Mason's eyes darted to another window. He shifted, putting himself between that one and the children.

Then they looked in a new direction, this time behind them. Dillion and Ivy kept searching for what worried them.

Then, out in the storm, lightning crackled overhead. The gloom illuminated.

A dozen figures appeared out of the shadows, surrounding the diner on all sides, blocking every escape.

"Too many," Mason said, forming another ball of heavenly flame in his other hand.

"Get toward the back," Everlee told the children.

The figures outside were clearer now as they approached. Dillion and Ivy could see their white, hungry eyes. They were living, vicious shadows.

As the foursome got as far from the windows as they could, the wraiths came right up to the glass, but not any further.

"What are they waiting for?" Mason asked.

Everlee looked back and forth. For a moment, she looked just as confused, as well.

Then her green eyes widened. She turned toward the children.

Something exploded from the back of the diner. A feral howl split the silence. Three wraiths poured through the back door, leaping across the tables toward them.

Everlee swung her fiery sword and bisected a wraith into

smoke. Mason hurled a flaming ball at another, forcing the third to scramble back in retreat. He spun again and threw the second bolt of light, this time at the glass, which shattered on impact and burst outward, showering the wraiths beyond in heated, shrapnel glass.

The third wraith tackled him while he was distracted.

"Stay down!" Everlee warned the kids. She held her sword with both hands and swung in a wide arc. She tore through one shadowy creature, swung again, and warded off the rest. The things didn't dare come closer. The more she slashed and hacked, the more they retreated. Despite their numbers, there wasn't enough space to get past her.

A wraith slammed into the ceiling, blasted off by Mason's heavenfire, and disintegrated. He jumped to his feet, his face marred by a long cut across one cheek. He summoned his own sword of flame and hacked apart another wraith.

But more continued pouring in.

Everlee and Mason stayed together, but they were outnumbered. Even the one here and there they managed to kill could be replaced by two or three more.

Everlee extended a free hand and poured flame from her fingertips, creating an arc of blue-white fire that formed a barrier between the crowd of wraiths and them. She and Mason were able to retreat from the fight, but the wraiths remained.

"It won't hold forever!" she warned over the roar. She looked exhausted. Her eyes were burning, as were Mason's. The more they used their fire, the more it seemed to take out of them. "We need help!"

"There isn't any," Mason reminded her. He unfurled a ball of flame and bolted it across the diner, striking one wraith off a table.

"We need to do something, then!"

"Like what?"

She was breathing heavy. Her worried eyes fell on the children, then on Mason, and then around them. She looked for a way out, but none appeared. Even if they went out the back, there could be more of them. And the wraiths knew they had them cornered. None were fleeing the heavenfire that engulfed the diner. They waited for their prey.

Something shot from beyond her wall of fire and Everlee her in the arm. A flash of orange and she screamed. Hellfire burned through her jacket at the shoulder. She faltered.

The heavenfire wall dimmed.

Mason covered her. He launched a jet of blue fire, but even he couldn't hold it for long.

"We're running out of time!" he warned, cradling her against him. Her sword extinguished. She could barely lift her arm. "Look, if we charge through them, keep the kids close to us, maybe we could—!"

She shook her head adamantly. "No!" she pushed him away and stood. "It won't work. The moment we get past that barrier, they'll swarm us."

"That barrier is collapsing, Everlee. If it comes down, it won't

130

matter."

"I know." She stood up fully, reigniting her blade. "I'm going to draw them in. When I do, you go through the thinnest spot in the horde. Get them out of here."

"And leave you?"

"Yes."

"No!" he shook his head. "Like hell I will!"

"You get them out! One of them is a Nephilim. Save them both, and at least one new Nephilim has a chance. Maybe even the shade, too!"

"Everlee!"

"Damnit, Mason, do what I tell you!"

Groaning in anger, he turned back toward the kids. He got down on a knee in front of them. "Look, one of you is a Nephilim. One of you has heavenfire. If you use it, we can scare them off."

"Mason, no! They're kids!" Everlee protested.

"We don't have any other option, Everlee!" he said to the two again. "Now, think: which one of you used their powers? Which one can use heavenfire?"

Dillion and Ivy were terrified. Neither could move. They were paralyzed by fear.

"Please, we're going to die if you don't tell me!"

The wraiths behind them howled. The flames were low enough that one attempted to jump over, but caught fire and burnt to ash. But the others were more patient.

Mason looked to Dillion. "You tried to fight before. It has to be you."

Dillion shook his head. "I don't know what I am doing!"

"You reach inside yourself," Mason told him, "and you find that part of you that's more than human. You find it, you call on it, and you use it." He took his hand and held it out. "Just like this. Release it. The fire will come."

"Mason, they're coming!" Everlee warned, her voice straining with pain. The flames got lower. "They can't help! We need to hold them off on our own!"

"He can do it!" Mason shouted.

Then, the flames flickered low, until they couldn't hold any longer. The wraiths poured over like a dark wave.

Mason leapt up, lashing out with his fiery sword. "Do it, Dillion!"

Dillion cried, hand shaking.

"Do it! Do it now, or we all die!"

Everlee swung and slashed with his good hand, cutting apart a wraith, but another grabbed her around the waist. Mason cut it apart, but one leapt to his back. The tide was about to roll over them.

Dillion sobbed futility.

Then, something like a mini-sun exploded through the diner. Like dawn, it swept outward with tongues of flame and light, curling through the tables and sweeping up wraiths in its path. Fire and warmth enveloped them, consumed them, and kept going. The one on Mason tried to run, but burnt into nothing. One had Everlee pinned, but disappeared in the starburst. The shadows evaporated.

Dillion fell to the ground, shielding his eyes. When he peered through his fingers, his vision adjusted, and floating in the middle of the new sun was Ivy. Her eyes burned white-hot. Fire flowed out of her, chasing the last remaining wraiths from the diner.

And then, just as suddenly, it all collapsed back within her. Flames extinguished. She dropped from inches off the ground to the tile. Dillion was there, catching her.

Silence enveloped the diner. All that remained was the crackle of the remaining flames and the heavy breathing of the survivors.

***

Dillion walked with Everlee. Mason carried Ivy. They were alive. But even cradled in Mason's arms, the girl would not let go of Dillion's hand. No matter that she protected them, she kept her fingers entwined in his, like he had done with hers. Protective. Secure. She insisted that even though he was a shade, he would come with them.

"Ever seen a new Nephilim do that?" Everlee asked Mason.

He shook his head. "Never seen any Nephilim do that."

"How did she?"

"No idea."

Everlee considered the sleeping child; so innocent, so harmless looking. She was anything but.

"Our powers come from our father," Everlee said. "It makes you wonder."

"About what?"

"About who her father is."

FAILED SUMMONING

GABBY GILLIAM

I summoned Mal by accident. I've never been good at spellcasting. I excel at herbology. My potions flawless. I can identify plants by their leaves and blossoms. Gathering necessary spell supplies is the easy part. Measuring the herbs calms me, a welcome distraction from what's to come.

Language derails my efforts every time. Mother laments my ineptitude. As leader of the coven, it is an embarrassment to have me for a daughter. The girl who sets her hair alight when trying to light a candle. The girl who dyes her skin blue when attempting a simple glamor spell.

Private tutors quit in frustration. I am unable to be taught.

I practice for hours every night once my mundane homework is complete. I recite incantations while the moon rises. Listen to recordings abandoned by my tutors when they declared my case to be hopeless. I match tone and pronunciation. Watch the way my mouth forms words in the mirror. As soon as I add ingredients, it all goes up in smoke. Most of the time, literally. We have fire extinguishers in every room in the house. We have yet to own one that reaches its expiration date without needing to be used.

I dug through tomes, searching for a spell that was foolproof. Easy words. Manageable ingredients. I found what I sought in a grimoire penned by my Great Aunt Claire. A southern belle at the turn of the century, she entertained often. She devised a spell to summon lemons to concoct her famous lemonade. Perfect ripeness. Seedless. Available every season, so she never had to disappoint a thirsty guest. The necessary ingredients adjusted to scale based on how many lemons you wanted to conjure. I focused on one. Start small, I figured. Less room for errors. Best of all, everything I needed for the spell was easy to find and acquire without raising my mother's suspicion or cautious hope. Should I fail, at least I alone would be there to witness it.

1 tsp. dried lemon peel

¼ c. water

½ tsp. vinegar

4 yellow candles

1 glass bowl, preferably clear

Combine first ingredients until peel is completely dissolved. Pour into a bowl. Place bowl in the center of pentagram drawn for your summoning circle. Place one yellow candle at each of the four compass points: North, South, East, and West. Facing East, chant the incantation: *Et sie a citrea.*

Four small words.

"You can do this," I whispered, trying to funnel courage into my shaking fingers.

I lit the four candles, honoring each of the elements in their turn. I called the quarters—North for earth, East for air, South for fire, West for water—to bring me the protection of the elements during my practice. I could use all the help they could provide. I set a clear Pyrex bowl in the circle. Then I closed my eyes and chanted in Latin.

"Et sie a citrea." I said the incantation three times. Always the power of three to strengthen my intention.

I knew as soon as I smelled sulfur that something had

gone wrong. Again. I sighed without opening my eyes.

"Fudge," I muttered. I huffed, sending my breath toward the summoning circle, indifferent to whether I blew out the candles. I didn't plan to try again tonight. I'd save that disappointment for another day.

I opened my eyes to find two fiery orange irises glaring back at me.

A demon perched over the glass bowl. The fiery eyes were a dead giveaway. The curves of his bare pectorals and abs were less expected. My mouth and throat were suddenly dry.

"Oh," I squeaked before my mouth failed me completely.

"Oh, indeed," the demon mused. "Care to tell me what I'm doing here?" he asked. His tone was cordial enough, but the heat of his gaze proved he didn't appreciate being summoned to my bedroom.

"You're not a lemon," I stammered, inching backward from the circle until the edge of my bed bit into my back.

The demon looked down as if seeing himself for the first time and then slowly raised his eyes to mine.

"It would appear the lady is correct," he said. One of his black eyebrows twitched. "Were you expecting something a bit more citrusy? Lemons aren't in season, you know?"

"B-b-but the spell was for lemons," I sputtered. My

bottom lip trembled. I bit it to keep it steady.

"It would seem you got more than you bargained for."

"Just go back to wherever you came from," I said.

"That's not really how this works," he said. Amusement crept into the edges of his words. "Humans summon demons and we make a bargain. I give you what you want in exchange for something I want."

"I don't want anything," I mumbled, unconvincing even to myself.

The demon tsked. "Everyone wants something."

"I just want you to leave," I said, waving my hand as if I could will him to disappear. It worked just about as well as any other spell I attempted.

"Yes, well, even if I were so inclined—which I'm not— it wouldn't be possible. Plus, I would have wasted an entire trip. Crossing through a portal into the mortal realm isn't a vacation. Not the most comfortable means of transport."

"What do you mean, it's not possible?" I asked. The demon gestured to the summoning circle.

"The pentagram holds me temporarily in place, but the candles are the waypoints of the portal. As you can see, their flames have gone out. The portal is no longer open."

"Can't you just teleport yourself back or something?"

"Usually, yes. That brings us back to the pentagram you

so cleverly drew on the floor here. It has a magic of its own. One that binds me here."

"For how long?" I asked, failing to mask the panic fluttering in my chest. The last word barreled out of me in a pitch only dogs could hear.

"It should wear off in a few days," he said without concern. As if this sort of thing happened to him all the time.

"A few days?" I repeated, panic stripped away by the irrationality of his words. "So, you'll just sit here. In my room. For days."

"It would appear so," the demon said. "I don't suppose you would like to make a bargain in the meantime? I have come all this way, after all." He batted his eyelashes at me. I didn't think anyone but cartoon characters actually did that.

"Not a chance, pal," I said. I began to pace my cramped bedroom. "How am I going to explain this to my mother?" I lamented. There's no way I could keep a demon a secret. What was I supposed to do, toss a blanket over his head and hope she'd think he was a pile of laundry?

"Another failure!" I threw my hands into the air in frustration, then turned and flopped onto my bed, face-first. "She's going to kill me," I muttered into my comforter. I'd broken one of my mother's only two rules. I'd summoned a demon into my bedroom. And it wasn't even on purpose.

"This happen a lot then?" the demon asked.

"Summoning demons? No," I said without lifting my head. "Making a huge mess of things? All the puffing time."

"I see. I could offer you some assistance," he hedged. "For a small fee."

"Not interested. I've made enough of a mess here. I'm not mucking it up any further."

"Just thought I would offer," he said, opening his hands in concession.

"So, you're really stuck here for days?" I asked, lifting my head so I could see him. He nodded. "Lovely," I said. I pushed myself up and began to gather my spellcasting supplies. I resisted the urge to chuck Aunt Claire's grimoire into the garbage.

"I don't even like lemons," I said as I threw the ill-fated book onto my bed.

"Why conjure one then?" the demon asked.

"It was supposed to be easy," I said, throwing the candles into my nightstand drawer so forcefully that one of them broke in half. "It was only four words, for crying out loud. Only I could mess up such a simple casting."

"A fledgling caster?" he mused. "I don't know whether to be offended or impressed."

"How could you possibly be either of those?" I asked in

surprise. I was offended by my lack of skill, but what could the demon find offensive about this situation?

"Summoning a demon is complex magic," he said. "Usually only a caster of great skill can perform the ritual with success. Thus, I'm impressed a fledgling could do it. What's offensive is that a caster with such a self-described lack of skill was able to pull me through the veil. I must be losing my touch." He wore a serious expression, but his eyes betrayed his amusement.

"Fledgling I am, and fledgling I'm doomed to stay." I picked the grimoire back up, only to set it back down on my dresser. None of the spells it contained would be of use to me. The book knocked over my jewelry tree, but I didn't bother to pick up the necklaces. I sank back into my bed, eyes staring up at the old star stickers on my ceiling. I had meticulously placed each sticker, so they made my favorite constellations.

"My mother hopes I'll complete my trials next week and become a full member of the coven." I tossed my words toward Orion's Belt, indifferent to whether the demon was listening or not, but somehow I knew he was.

"A witch's trial requires a display of skills in all disciplines," I continued. "If I could choose to brew a potion or recite the properties of herbs, I could pass easily enough.

I've no doubt any attempt at casting will hoffiry the coven. My mother will be humiliated. The coven will deny my bid for membership and my mother will be forced to choose between me and them."

"Do you worry she will not choose you?" the demon asked. "Is that the cause of your distress?"

I snorted. "I have no doubts regarding her choice. She barely tolerates me as it is. She'll be rid of me soon enough."

"Are you so certain she will choose coven over kin?"

"She's the head of the coven. She would never give up so much power." I shook my head. "I know what her choice will be. I've always known."

The demon raised his hands and touched the tips of his fingers together, considering me over the tented shape they made.

"Next week, you say? Samhain?"

I nodded. "One of the nights our powers are strongest. It gives the fledglings a chance to display their skill to maximum effect. My mother conjured a white stag at her trial. Then, she hunted it down and placed its warm corpse at the coven leader's feet. They feasted on its flesh that night. It was a sign of how great she would become."

"A bit over the top, if you ask me," the demon said. I couldn't believe he would dismiss her skill so quickly. "She tried too hard. Seems to be a family trait." He raised an eyebrow and smirked at me.

"I don't think I'm trying hard enough," I said, unable to believe he would compare my failure to conjure a lemon to my mother's spectacular display of skill at her trial.

"You think too much. That's the problem."

"You've known me for all of ten minutes," I said, sitting up and glaring at him across my footboard. "How could you possibly know anything about me or my problems?"

"The best practitioners I've ever seen make the art look effortless," he said.

"Don't you think I know that?" I threw my hands in the air and my body from the bed, marching toward the summoning circle, my finger pointed at him like it could cut him down. "I've watched my mother for years, the way the magic pours from her, as easy as breathing. I'll never control my casting the way she does." I stopped with my finger inches from his nose, my chest heaving.

"Bring me a candle," he said, unaffected by my threatening finger.

"What? Why?" I asked, dropping my hand to my side.

"Just fetch me one."

I walked to my nightstand and grabbed one of the yellow candles. I stomped back over to him and slapped it into his outstretched hand.

"Light it," he said, holding the candle up.

"I would have brought matches if you'd told me you needed it lit," I barked. "Light it yourself." I was done with his games. Done with this day.

"You don't need matches," he said.

"Right. It's just going to light itself is it?" I asked, irritation raising my voice in both pitch and volume. I'd tried this trick hundreds of times, most of which ended in me setting myself on fire. "Or maybe I'll just snap my fingers, and it will light like magic, right?" I snapped my fingers in his face, my mouth twisted into a near snarl. I had struggled with casting my whole life, and this demon thought he could mock me for it?

A flame appeared, so close to my hair that I pulled back, afraid my head would catch fire. The demon's eyes danced in the light.

"See," he said. "You think too much."

"You probably lit it yourself," I said, unwilling to believe I could control even that simple bit of magic.

"Scout's honor," he said, raising three clawed fingers into the air. "And I bet you could do it again. Here." He pinched the flame between his thumb and forefinger. "Try again."

"It's a waste of time," I said. "I didn't even say a spell.

Whatever magic caused that flame didn't come from me."

"You didn't need to say a spell because your intention was clear. Try. Again." He held the candle up. I glared at him. I didn't know what game he was playing, and I didn't like being the butt of whatever joke this was to him.

I stared at the smoking wick and thought, "*ignis,*" ready to prove the demon wrong. Another flame leapt up. I sat back on my heels, staring at it in surprise.

"How?" I asked the demon.

"You learned to get out of your own way," he said.

"Your insight is invaluable. I should have summoned you ages ago," I told him with an exaggerated roll of my eyes. But I was enjoying myself. It was nice to feel something other than the sting of failure. That fluttering in my stomach each time the flame appeared, I think it might have been hope.

SINS OF THE FATHER

ELLEN ROSE

London,

The Museum of Mythology.

"He's here again," whispered Kelly.

"Really?" asked Diana.

Kelly's eyebrows raised at her co-worker's eagerness. "You want to watch yourself, love. It's close to becoming stalking at this point. You want to watch that he doesn't follow you home." She chuckled.

"Shh," Dinna scolded. Perhaps she should be frightened

of this man, how could someone be so interested in her small museum that it brought them in everyday for the past week? Granted, she found mythology fascinating, but she'd yet to meet anyone else who matched her level of fascination on the subject. Kelly couldn't care less, she was more interested in painting her nails and gabbing about her latest date, but people weren't exactly lining up to work here. The museum was a labour of love for Diana, especially as her Medieval Mythology PhD was getting her nowhere on the job front.

She glanced at herself in the mirror. She had taken greater care with her appearance today, taming her wild copper curls, and sweeping mascara over her eyelashes to accentuate her big, blue eyes.

She cleared her throat. "Good morning, sir. Can I help you with anything?" she asked, her voice quaking slightly.

His eyes widened; these were the first words she had spoken to him all week. "No, thank you." He smiled, walking towards the front desk. "Diana, is it?"

"Wh-what? How do you know my name?"

He grinned. "Your name-tag."

"Oh!" she flushed. "Yes, of course."

Up close he was even more perfect. He was the tallest man she had ever seen, with rippling muscles that appeared perfectly carved. He wore his hair long, jet-black and glistening.

"I'm Ben, pleased to meet you," he said, extending his hand.

Diana took it, gasping at his strength, and the buzz of electricity she felt when they were intertwined. Dropping her hand, he hung his head. "Sorry about that," he said quietly.

"It's no problem, really. May I ask what brings you here? It's just, we don't get many visitors and you've been here an awful lot this week."

He chuckled. "Yes, I have, haven't I? I suppose I just feel drawn here."

"Oh, do you now?" said Kelly, returning from her smoke break, raising her eyebrows suggestively at Diana.

Diana felt warmth cover her cheeks. "I'll show you around," she smiled, leading Ben away from the watchful eyes of Kelly.

They moved together around the small museum, going on a journey from Ancient Greek mythology, and ending with Chinese folklore. He listened diligently, while Diana explained the exhibits and artifacts on display behind glass cases. He nodded and murmured in agreement as she whittled off some of her facts, staring intently at her face.

"I must say, I greatly admire your passion. What sparked your interest in all of this?" he asked, gesturing to the exhibits.

Diana went quiet, and bit at her lip. "To be completely honest, I don't know," she said, shrugging her shoulders. The truth was, she felt drawn to mythology, a deep love for it, before she ever truly knew anything about it. If fate and prophecies were to be believed, then she supposed that there was a higher plan, that it was her destiny to continue her research.

A sad, far-off look passed over Ben's face like a dark cloud sneaking across the sky. He gently stroked his fingers over one of the glass cases, peering in closely at a mummified child's body. "Do you feel like that sometimes? Stuck behind a cage with everyone looking in at you and you can do nothing about it? And that trying to resist is futile?"

Diana's mouth opened in shock. Not at the seemingly odd sentence this stranger had uttered to her, but because she finally felt understood. Before she could answer, he scanned her face and shook his head apologetically.

"I'm sorry, forgive me. I don't know where that came from," he said, walking to the exit. With his hand on the door, he looked back, and with a sad smile whispered "Goodbye, Diana."

The rest of the day dragged on, and Diana found herself drifting off into a beautiful daydream, filled with mystical creatures, beating wings, and desire. *Was she going mad? Had all this mythology study left her living in her own fantasy world?*

"Hello!" said Kelly, clicking her fingers in front of Diana's face. "Did you not hear me? I said I'm leaving; I have a date! Sam again, he's taking me for sushi. Will you be okay locking up?"

"Yes, sorry. See you tomorrow, enjoy your date."

Diana locked up the museum and pulled on her winter coat. The rain was beating down, and the inky black sky was lit up furiously by a bolt of lightning. Feeling wary of the London streets at night, Diana sprinted to her car. She rang out her dripping wet hair and removed her coat, which at this point was doing more harm than good. The engine ticked over as she began her usual route home. The roads were deserted. This sent shockwaves through her body, and, her hands shaking, she sped up. As the lightning once again pierced the sky, it illuminated a dark figure. Diana screamed and swerved the car, skidding to an abrupt halt. She looked in the rear-view mirror.

No, she wasn't going mad. There was someone... something in the centre of the road. Diana squinted, and then gasped as she watched the figure align clearly in her field of vision. It was Ben, but he was a great deal taller, and every inch of him was crackling and pulsating with electricity, turning his body purple. Sprouted from his back were feathered white angel wings.

She climbed out of the car.

He locked eyes with her. "Don't be frightened, please, Diana."

That magnetic pull had returned, leading her towards him. "I'm not afraid of you," she whispered, and the words seemed to calm him.

"Don't cry," she said, wiping a tear from his face.

Her memories were gradually beginning to return to her, trickling through her mind like a stream of water.

"I'm remembering," she whispered. "I loved you and you loved me, but you left me. You left us behind, why?"

He took her hand. "Believe me, I did everything I could *not* to leave you." He sighed. "Your memories will still be fuzzy, there's a spell blocking them. A spell that my father implanted in your mind. We met years ago at university. I wanted to live a normal life, away from the toxic rule of my father. He banished me, although I knew it wouldn't last. I'm his sole heir to the kingdom, and he's too old to father another child. You felt connected to me because we've loved each other for ten years. When my father's spies reported this back to him, his lightning bolts cracked the sky and fell onto Earth, threatening to rip it to shreds. I had to return to the Heavens, I had no choice."

"I understand, I understand completely," Diana replied.

"Thank you. I knew you would, you encouraged me to go back up, you couldn't risk the lives of millions for the sake of our love, no matter how powerful." He squeezed her hand. "I'm a Nephilim. My father is Zeus, and my mother is a mortal woman. They fell in love, and she bore me. My father took my mother and I to the Heavens, where my grandfather executed my mother without a moment's hesitation. Despite my grandfather's rage at my father poisoning the bloodline, I was to be raised in the Heavens as his heir and when I came of age, I was to marry a pure-blood goddess. That, obviously, was not to happen." He smiled softly at Diana, tucking a strand of hair behind her ear.

"But that's not what the history states, aren't Nephilim supposed to be monstrous giants who are confined to the Heavens?"

He chuckled. "No, that's what the rulers wish you to believe. In reality we are much more like mortals, only in our true form we are fallen angels with a connection to both the mortal realm and the Heavens."

Diana's thoughts were buzzing so quickly that it pained her. She took a deep breath and clasped her thumb and forefinger over the bridge of her nose. "What now, Ben? What do we do now? You know that your father won't let us be together."

"I need to take my place as ruler and re-write these ancient blood rules. I need to remove my father from the throne…perhaps even to kill him."

Diana gasped.

"He is no father of mine, Diana. Nor any kind or just ruler to the people. They do not love him. He is a cruel, poisonous God. A God who tortured his own son for years as punishment, both leading me from you and…" he turned around, and lifting his wings, showed Diana the deep, ribbed scars from the brutal lashings of thousands of whips. Diana ran her fingers over the scars with tears pooling in her eyes.

"They will accept me, I have many allies in the kingdom who will fight for me, fully aware of the consequences. But I need something from you," he said.

"Anything," Diana replied.

"A weapon. One that I hid in your museum many moons ago. If wielded correctly, it can defeat Zeus."

They returned to the museum, and Diana followed Ben to her small storeroom. He punched through the ceiling and into a crawlspace. With rubble falling around his shoulders, he yanked down a thin, steel sword.

Diana gasped, taking it from him. She turned it over in her hands and, giggling excitedly, squealed, "The Sword of the Ancients!"

"You know about the sword?"

"Of course, any mythology graduate worth her salt knows of the sword – I thought it was a myth! Anyone worthy of the sword may wield it and rule the Heavens," she said, handing the sword back to her love. "You're worthy. I know, I can just feel it."

Ben smiled, wrapping his arms and angel wings around her petite frame. "Are you ready?"

She nodded, hanging onto him for dear life.

"It's time to go to the sky," he said, bending his knees and taking flight into the Heavens.

***

It's all real, Diana thought, her eyes darting around the Heavens. *It's all real*. Lightning cracked against the sky. The dark clouds outlined the Great Hall. There were long blue tables, decorated with ornate gold and silver. Gods and goddesses sat on marble chairs, dining and laughing. Sitting on the throne was Zeus himself in all his majesty, his white beard and wrinkled face giving the impression of knowledge and power, and yet, Diana realised with surprise, weakness, perhaps even sadness. The room fell silent, as thousands of

155

pairs of eyes fell on their guests. Two stone dogs began to roar and bare their teeth.

Zeus raised one finger. "Heel," he commanded, and the dogs returned to statutes. "My *son*," he said, his tone seeped in sarcasm. "How dare you show your face in my kingdom. And with the mortal scum, I see. Have you learned nothing?"

His eyes scanned his son and settled upon the sword. A laugh so deep, so maniacal, escaped his lips that Diana backed herself up into the corner of the hall.

"Oh, my son, do you believe that you are worthy of the sword? It's a death sentence for those unworthy who dare to brandish it."

The two were walking together as they talked. The mighty weight of them shook the floor. Ben fell onto one knee, holding out the sword.

"Of course, father."

Zeus snatched the sword and kicked Ben with about as much force as a human would swat away a fly. For any mortal, or part mortal, this kick was enough to crush bone. Ben flew back into a pillar with a sickening crack.

"No!" Diana cried, running towards him, but Ben threw up his hand to stop her.

"I'm sorry it had to end like this, but you are no son of mine. And you and your future spawn will never rule this kingdom," said Zeus, bringing down the sword and attempting to thrust it into Ben's heart. The force of the sword threw Zeus back with the power of his own lightning bolt, the steel burning into his hands. He cried out as Ben limped over to him and picked up the sword.

"Unworthy," he said, staring down at him. "The sword has deemed you to be unworthy, father." He looked around the room, the subjects stunned into silence. "With the power of the Ancients, I hereby banish you, unworthy God, to the mortal realm. You will be stripped of your powers and will live out the remainder of your days in exile."

He turned to Aliya, the Goddess of Magic. "Will you please do the honours, Goddess?"

Diana gasped as her eyes took in the most beautiful creature, with long white hair and a soft glow to her features. "With pleasure," she smiled.

"You haven't heard the last of me, boy," Zeus spat, as he signalled for his three most loyal subjects. They placed protective arms over their king, as they disappeared in a puff of smoke to cheers and celebrations.

"I'm going to be making a few changes around here." He smiled at his subjects, his eyes settling on Diana. He gestured for her to come and join him. "Allow me to introduce you to Diana, and the woman soon to be your Queen, should she accept me, of course."

Diana answered him by planting her lips over his, to the cheers of everyone in the kingdom.

They bowed eagerly to their new rulers; the poison fully eradicated from the Heavens.

ABOUT THE AUTHORS

Barend Nieuwstraten III grew up and lives in Sydney, Australia, where he was born to Dutch and Indian immigrants. He has worked in film, short film, television, music, and online comics. He is now primarily working on a collection of stories set within a high fantasy world, a science fiction alternate future, as well as a steampunk storyverse, often dipping his toes in horror in the process.

With over twenty stories published in anthologies, he continues to work on short stories, stand-alone novels, and an epic series.

A discovery writer not knowing what will happen when he begins typing, he endeavours to drag his readers on the

same unknown journey through the fog of his
subconscious.

Facebook: https://www.facebook.com/Barend3Author

Twitter: barend3@barend3Author

[https://twitter.com/Barend3Author]

Blog: https://barend3.blogspot.com

B.F. Vega is a writer, poet, and theater artist living in the
North Bay Area of California. Her short stories and poetry
have appeared in Nightmare Whispers, Dark Celebration,
Sage Cigarettes, The Cauldron Anthology, The Literary
Nest and 'Fae Dreams'. She is still shocked when people
refer to her as an author---every time.
You can follow her on Facebook: @B.F.Vegaauthor and on
Twitter: @ByronWhoKnew.

Born in the shadow of the grand metropolis of Chicago,
D.L. Smith-Lee is a lifelong lover of fantasy and science
fiction. His published works include short stories of horror
and dark fantasy with Sirens Call Publications, Zimbell
House Publishing, The Were-Traveler, J.A. Mes Press,
Black Hare Press, Roaring Lions Productions' Rococoa

anthology, and Scout Media's A Haunting of Words anthology. He resides in Chicago where he is a Master of Fine Arts candidate at Chicago State University.

http://www.facebook.com/dlsmithlee

Ellen Rose is a romance writer from England. In her spare time she enjoys reading, hiking, and spending time with her loved ones.

Emily Sharp is a British born New Zealand writer. She attends the University of Canterbury in Christchurch, currently studying a double major in English and Classics, looking to complete a Masters. Her work is mainly short fiction or poetry. Her writing centres on creating and re-creating myths, legends, and ideas around anthropology and culture. She enjoys experimenting with pseudo-scientific anthropology and combining it with deity and origin myth. To remain credible when writing on historical events and civilisations she ensures the topic is heavily studied, critiqued and compared with peer-reviewed and primary sources before embarking. Emily writes and creates these pieces with the aim of stimulating imagination and encouraging conversation. Especially around myths, beliefs and history which have more than meets the eye and parallel occurrences across cultures. Emily will continue to create content in this field with the hope that it will inspire and entertain readers.

Gabby Gilliam lives in the DC metro area. Her poetry has most recently appeared in *Tofu Ink, The Ekphrastic Review, Cauldron Anthology, Instant Noodles, MacQueen's Quinterly,* and *Equinox.* Her short fiction has appeared in collections from Black Hare Press and Iron Faerie Publishing. You can find her online at gabbygilliam.squarespace.com or on Facebook at www.facebook.com/GabbyGilliamAuthor.

Jessica Turnbull is an author who mainly writes Young Adult Fantasy. However, she is hoping to also branch into Sci-Fi, Horror and New Adult. Books got her through her darkest years as a teenager, and she hopes that one day her books will inspire young people to keep going. She lives in the UK with her two cats, Rocky and Mishka.

Links (just two):

Jordan Davidson is a Humanities student at Yale University, which basically means that she's somehow made it so that she can major in fantasy. Her work has been previously published in Class Collective, The Common Tongue, and Youth Imagination.

Spencer Helsel is an American author from Virginia who has spent the last decade teaching in the continental United States and abroad. He holds a B.A. in English Literature and Education from Christopher Newport University, is a member of the Sigma Tau Delta English Honors Society, and has self-published three fantasy novels, with plans to expand into other genres. He currently lives with his wife Jessica and three sons wherever the U.S. military sends them.

Of Indian origin, Sultana Raza's poems/fiction/CNF have appeared in 100+ journals. SFF work: Entropy, Columbia Journal, Star*line, Bewildering Stories, Focus & Vector (BSFA), Unlikely Stories Mark V, Galaxy#2 #4, #5, Antipodean SF and File770.

Her fiction received an Honorable Mention in Glimmer Train Review. Also published in Coldnoon Journal, Knot Literature, and Setu. She's read her fiction/poems in Switzerland, France, Luxembourg, England, Ireland, the USA, WorldCon 2018, and CoNZealand 2019.

Her creative non-fiction will/has appeared in Literary Ladies Guide, Literary Yard, Litro, impspired, Dream Pop Journal (in 2023) etc. An independent scholar, Sultana Raza's presented papers on Romanticism (Keats) and Fantasy (Tolkien) in international conferences.

Made in the USA
Las Vegas, NV
28 April 2024